Big Adventure *on* Moa Nui

The Very

MYSTERIOUS EVENTS

on a

SOUTH PACIFIC ISLAND

and

THEIR RESOLUTION

A Fiona Elizabeth Kelly Adventure

BY LLYN DE DANAAN

Copyright © 2011 LLyn De Danaan
All rights reserved.
ISBN: 1466267054
ISBN-13: 9781466267053
Library of Congress Control Number: 2011915410
CreateSpace, North Charleston, SC

For Sally and Marilyn

With many thanks to the people
who introduced me to
life in the South Pacific.
Special thanks to Frederique, Marty, Moe,
Emere, Randi, and Jimmy

Thanks also to the Gromiteers and family
And to all my "fellow travellers"

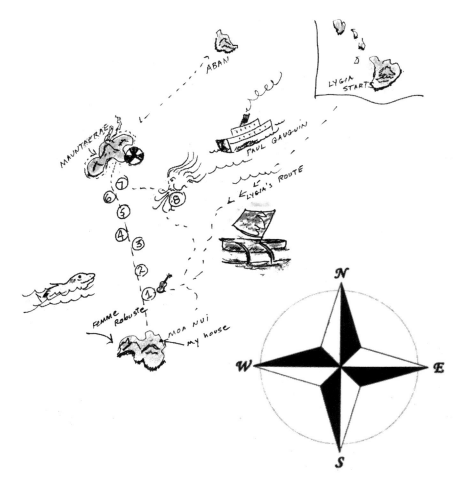

A rough map from Kelly's field notebook showing approximate route of the journey to and from Mauntaerae from Moa Nui as well as estimated location of sightings mentioned in Gertrude's "Odyssey."

MAP KEY:
1. Approximate point that Lygia came aboard. Also note the intersection of Paul Gauguin with Lygia's journey.
2. Sperm Whale!!
3. Floating Mouths and Drumming Moths encountered
4. Smiling Pickerels and Shell Encrusted Albatross encountered
5. Vengeful Pomeranians and Plover with Claw Like Fang encountered
6. Mildewed Dolphin and Disappearing Fish
7. Frozen Walrus and Mites encountered
8. Cyclone on way home

Nuclear symbol is location of Mauntaerae

DRAMATIS PERSONAE

Fiona "Kelly" Elizabeth Kelly: Intuitive anthropologist and narrator. Reliable? Your call.

Anna Marie: The proprietor of *Kilter Line Prophecy and Liberation Astrology*.

Deena Serene: The translator who worked with "Kelly" as she interviewed islanders.

Lygia: A skillful cellist from Fogo Island, Newfoundland.

Anui: A resident of Moa Nui and a masterful crafts person and navigator.

Aban: A Malayo-Polynesian from an unknown island who has heard a call he must answer.

Gertrude: Raised by "traditional" aunties and uncles, she composes and chants to people and animals.

Emere: Excellent marks-person and home decorator. Her ties to a grandmother warrior give her strength. Also sells *Avon* products.

Phad: A brave companion dog named after his owners' favorite Thai noodle dish.

Henri: A boulanger fabuleux (terrific baker) who knows how to put a saucier to good use. Co-owner, with Loretta, of the restaurant, *Le Grand Thon* (The Big Tuna).

Loretta: Partner of Henri in many ventures. Can dance, sing, cook, play a saxophone, and walk a tight rope.

Jean-Louis: Proprietor of Kelly's rental home and good man.

Lucretia: "Kelly's" cat who, though seldom present in the narrative, certainly is on Kelly's mind throughout her journey.

Henrietta Poussiere: Long dead anthropologist who studied in and wrote about Moa Nui.

Margaret Anderson: American spy in the 1920s whose statue stands in Besoin.

Hjordis Gumundsdottir: Local taxi driver and owner of Brazilian Jujitsu school.

Magnolia: *The* Chamber of Commerce of Moa Nui.

IMPORTANT LANDMARKS

Moa Nui: The island whose people call Kelly, the intuitive anthropologist, for help. Moa Nui is an independent republic, formerly a French protectorate. Population, according to most recent census: 6,742.

Besoin: The main town of the island. It is comprised of a two block line of small shops and eateries built along the coastline and behind the quay where cargo ships arrive weekly with goods from other islands.

Snack Shack: A casual place for a coffee, breakfast, or lunch to go. It serves as a community center, especially for women who come to town to shop. There are bulletin boards advertising items for sale or wanted. The shop owners maintain several small tables in front of the shop for selling or giving away small items such as blouses and baby clothes.

Chez Guillot's: A friendly pub

Le Grand Thon: A very nice restaurant and bakery owned by Lorretta and Henri

Chez Collette's: A nice coffee shop. It is more "upscale" than the Snack Shack. The owner advertises daily specials on signboards in front to attract the occasional tourist.

Aheihei: The capital of the French governed Aho Island chain located in the South Pacific.

Aohanqua: An island named for a kind of flax imported from New Zealand in the mid-1800s. It took over the island. It is one of the Aho Island chain, about a three day paddle from Mauntaerae.

Mauntaerae: The island lost to nuclear testing.

A FEW WORDS

Maeva: Welcome

Motu: General name for any series of coral islets separated from the main island

Quay: A wharf used as a landing place.

Ia ora na: Hello

Mauruuru roa: Thanks very much

Parang: Large knife or sword

Pareo: A Polynesian sarong, usually quite bright and flowery

CONTENTS

Chapter I	Arrival	1
Chapter II	Chien Perdu	9
Chapter III	The Dog with the Black Mask	13
Chapter IV	Glossolalia	19
Chapter V	My Job	23
Chapter VI	Maps in the Sand	31
Chapter VII	Kilter Line Prophecy and Liberation Astrology	33
Chapter VIII	The Work of an Anthropologist	39
Chapter IX	Stonefish Speaks	43
Chapter X	Interesting Facts About Moa Nui	51
Chapter XI	Preparation	59
Chapter XII	Anui	69
Chapter XIII	Gritty Sheets	77
Chapter XIV	Emere's Story	81
Chapter XV	Chicken *Fa Fa* and a Mission	87
Chapter XVI	Lest I Forget	93
Chapter XVII	Phad	95
Chapter XVIII	The Pits of Despair	99
Chapter XIX	More Pits	103
Chapter XX	Almost Ready to Go…But…	105
Chapter XXI	Ready to Go	109
Chapter XXII	Launch!	111
Chapter XXIII	A Warning: By Our New Companion	117
Chapter XXIV	Day One	119
Chapter XXV	Lygia Comes Aboard	123
Chapter XXVI	Gertrude Chants a Canoe Spell	129

Chapter XXVII	Day Two: In Which We Meet the Sperm Whale	131
Chapter XXVIII	Day Three: The Odyssey by Gertrude Set to Music by Lygia	135
Chapter XXIX	Day Four: How to Navigate a Canoe in the Pacific	139
Chapter XXX	Landing on Mauntaerae	141
Chapter XXXI	A Busy Morning	145
Chapter XXXII	The Long Climb to the Top	151
Chapter XXXIII	The Next Morning	155
Chapter XXXIV	The Trembling Earth	159
Chapter XXXV	On We Go	165
Chapter XXXVI	On the Beach	167
Chapter XXXVII	The Hole in the Center of the Earth	171
Chapter XXXVIII	Overcoming the Monster: Healing the Earth	177
Chapter XXXIX	Meanwhile, Back on the Beach	181
Chapter XXXX	From Evil, Beauty	183
Chapter XXXXI	Gertrude Rejoices	187
Chapter XXXXII	Back to Our Friends	189
Chapter XXXXIII	The Return	197
Chapter XXXXIV	Farewell to Moa Nui	203

Epilogue 207
Acknowledgments 213
Nuclear Testing in the Pacific 217
Disclaimer 219

PREFACE

This book is a spoof on sci fi, adventure, and mystery genres. Although it is meant to be a fun read, there are serious elements embedded in the text. Island people around the world have been colonized and ill treated for hundreds of years. Military needs of Western nations have often taken priority over the well being of indigenous people. For example, the British in the late 1960s and 70s relocated the population of the Chagos chain island, Diego Garcia, so that the U.S. could establish a base in the Indian Ocean. The descendents of these people still long to return.

More notorious than the Chagos incidents are the many nuclear tests conducted in the Pacific. The impacts of these are still felt. What follows, however, is fiction.

The astrological omens say you have the potential to see further and deeper into any part of reality you choose to focus on. Inner truths that have been hidden from you are ready to be plucked by your penetrating probes. For best results, cleanse your thoughts of expectations. Perceive what's actually there, not what you want or don't want to be there.

Fiona Elizabeth Kelly's horoscope the day she left for Moa Nui
Rob Brezsny, Freewill Astrology

CHAPTER I

Arrival

Imagination is more important than knowledge. For knowledge is limited to all we now know and understand, while imagination embraces the entire world, and all there ever will be to know and understand.
Albert Einstein

I could hardly unfold my body from a seated position after the cramped flight from L.A. to Moa Nui, but I didn't complain much. The destination almost always compensates for the journey. Things started to get interesting, even exotic, in L.A. I knew I was on a trip when I entered a big, dimly lit room near my gate. It had row after row of battered plastic chairs. I looked for an empty one in which to settle and wait for my outbound flight. It was a hopeless search, so I stood and looked around, taking in the scene. This end of the international terminal was so packed with Asian globetrotters that I could imagine I was in Guangzhou or Shanghai or Chongching even before I set foot on an airplane. The airport personnel called it a "lounge." Come on. A lounge is a place to relax, drape oneself on a cozy chair and happily slump, slouch, and flop. This place, with fetid air and hundreds of travelers, each hogging two or three stiff, unwelcoming seats—one for their socked feet, one for their oversized carry-ons, and one for their actual bodies—was more like an Italian refugee center. That is, it had the ambiance of those dismal tent cities where desperate boat people from North Africa are warehoused. Everyone seems despairing, homeless, and semi-drugged. And, as in the refugee centers, people were hugging their few, feeble belongings packed in threadbare knapsacks or scuffed vinyl suitcases. Some groups of people were gathered on the floor, like the patient economic migrants squatting on their belongings in front of the Beijing train station. These travelers were passing round cups of noodles and gobbling up contents with throwaway wooden chopsticks. There were also teenagers in stiff-billed, hip-hop style hats, men in business suits on cell phones, and old women in modern variations on the Chinese pajama theme. There were dozens of sleepy children with animal-patterned backpacks. People held cups of bad, cold coffee. Some youngsters played games on their iPads. A few people were fast asleep on the floor, heads supported by rolled up jackets and sweaters. Each person who was awake checked and rechecked tickets, fingered passports, and intermittently stared bleakly at the reader boards that announce departures and arrivals.

Airlines that I thought were long defunct were operating, stacked up waiting to pull in to the gates. Flights were announced every so often, but not often enough to satisfy anyone's hopes. Travelers were simply exhausted waiting for delayed flights.

Getting into the plane was not much of a relief. Hanging in the sky at 30,000 feet for eight or nine hours inside a flimsy, cramped Airbus over half a globe's worth of dark blue ocean glimpsed through scratched window panes is not my idea of a good time. Air Tahiti Nui seats are deceptive. We might just as well have been fitted with straight jackets as we enter the cabin. The back cushions looked inviting enough until I tried to actually get comfortable. They were hard and unforgiving, designed to hold the passengers still and upright in their assigned seats. The plane was only half full this trip, so, theoretically, one could stretch out. But it didn't do much good, because the arms between seats, fitted out with minimally functional remotes, didn't go all the way up. If I wanted to use the unoccupied seats next to me, I had to wedge my body between and under the obstacles present. The modest pillows that were issued by not surprisingly cranky attendants were not thick enough to cushion the arm on which I tried in vain to rest my head. A remote was tucked into the arm. It was there to be used to operate a small screen on the back of the seat in front of mine, but it didn't do much. When I jabbed at the button that draws it back into its niche, it lurched and then retracted violently. If one wasn't cautious, the damn thing could knock them out. Mine back to its resting place, narrowly missing my forehead. The next time I tried it, I was struck hard on the chin and decided not to touch it again. I slept occasionally though the stewards, like good nurses, woke me for feedings, usually just as I seemed to enter some wonderful, deep, place. Some of the offerings turned out to be quite tasty. The *plat principal* during the flight was *Raviolis au fromage de chèvre sauce à la tomate*. You don't get that on United. Or maybe that it was the French description that made it seem to be better than most airline fare.

Things looked up as the plane descended into Tahiti. How could they not? Two men played ukuleles as I walked from the tarmac to the terminal. One instrument was a Tahitian eight string, the other a four string. Strummed together, they made a uniquely beguiling, welcoming sound, and I began to relax and enjoy my sleep-deprived state. Women who carried baskets full of them gave a small frangipani blossom to each passenger. The scent of frangipani always has a soporific effect on me. I soon forgot all that I could complain about, including the sore shoulders and the heavy eyes. I was in the South Pacific. The sea was blue, the skies were open, and the world was at peace. Maybe.

The little jet prop that took me the rest of the way to Moa Nui could not tolerate much baggage. I was charged an extra 1500 Polynesian francs or "franis" (about $15 U.S.) for checking what had been my carry-on baggage, but I didn't mind, because, by the time I got to the check-in, I had been mesmerized, not only by the frangipani, but by the clicking of the overhead fans, a beat or so faster than my heart beat. It was the sound of the tropics, the one you count on hearing wherever you go in Southeast Asia or the South Pacific, unless you have enough money and poor judgment to stay in fancy hotels with air conditioning. The click-click of the fan blades going round and round over head is the sound of Singapore, of Belize, of rat hole rooming houses in Udaipur and beat up bars in southern Mexico. It is the sound of the old Raffles and the almost as old and not quite as appealing Aurora in Kuching, the Eastern and Oriental in Georgetown, Penang (near the best *roti cennai* stand in the world) and Langkawi. It evokes lime and tonic, the spicy fruit taste of Pimm's Cups and the smell of ground chilies and the smoky scent of spent Chinese firecrackers and Taoist temples. The air it stirs as it whirs about feels like an ocean breeze and its fins resemble the waving palms that line each water front inn and grace every courtyard. That is what turned the trip into an adventure: the sound of those clicking fans and the occasional scent of frangipani.

• • •

Moa Nui. I can't tell you exactly where it is, and I have even changed the name of the island to protect the privacy of it and the people who live there. It was colonized and ruled by the French for many years but became an independent republic some twenty years ago. I can tell you that, a long time ago the International Dateline was drawn right down the middle of Moa Nui. I didn't know much more about the complications that caused for everyone until later.

• • •

I can tell you that landing in Moa Nui was almost as much fun as landing in the old Hong Kong Kai Tak airport with that breathtakingly, hold your hat and say your rosary, low approach across Victoria Harbour. It was almost that much fun except, of course, there were no beyond-belief skyscrapers on the Moa Nui horizon or junks and sampans on the sea below. The strip in Moa Nui was, however, built on the edge of the ocean, inside the reef zone beyond which the waves break. You have to hit it right and you have to stop in time if you don't want to ditch. Maybe that was why the slick, in-flight magazine published regular articles touting the skill and long experience of their pilots. Passengers could feel safe knowing that these landings are being made by the best in the industry. All of these pilots knew what they were doing, including, maybe particularly, the four women captains. It was a short flight, forty-five minutes or so, from Papeete to Moa Nui. I left behind me, as the plane lifted off, the exquisitely beautiful, jagged, saw-toothed peaks of Tahiti. The flight crossed over miles of an ocean that sparkled with every shade of blue: from azure to electric to cobalt to teal and turquoise.

Moa Nui itself was a big circle of a dark green land mass surrounded by a lighter, greenish blue of lagoon and ringed by a thin white surf line. The very dark ultramarine blue of the deep ocean was beyond its reef, cut by two channels that were clearly marked for big boats to enter and exit. That first look at Moa Nui was simply stunning. It couldn't be more inviting from the air. And then one landed, if the air traffic controllers were awake. Planes came in so infrequently that it was hard for the people in the little tower to keep from being bored. One had figured out a way to fish from his post by cracking the window in front of his radar screen and tossing a long line out. There really was no "air traffic" to worry about. Scheduled landings came in only once every other day, and that depended on whether there were passengers on the other end and whether it was cyclone season. The closest the island had to an unscheduled landing was when Amelia Earhart was lost and controllers were put on alert. There weren't even scheduled visits in those days.

Moa Nui itself, once on the ground, was even more inviting than promised by web sites and tour books. I was feeling very lucky to have this job. I walked down the stairway that had been pulled up to the open door of the Air Tahiti ATR42 Turboprop and watched bemused as most of the other passengers waited by the cargo door as dozens of giant plastic coolers were unloaded. Each arriving passenger grabbed at least one. I found out later that this "luggage" served to carry special food items sent home with the passengers by relatives.

I retrieved my rolling duffle and backpack and wondered what next. I walked into the airport lobby and a group of people moved toward me. A muscled woman in a black tank top was in the lead. Her arms were covered with tattoos.

"Keel-eee?" she asked. She was accompanied by a slim, soft-spoken man in a floral shirt. There were others, apparently people who had hired me, who crowded around and gave me flowers and smiled. French and Tahitian flowed. I didn't understand one at all, the Tahitian, and got only a word or two of the other it was going by so quickly. I did "get" that I was needed and most welcome.

In the small crowd, I spotted a woman who looked familiar. It was Anna Marie, a local leader, "sensitive," and friend of a Naxi *Dongba* I'd worked with in Lijiang, China. She'd contacted me through him. A *Dongba* is what is commonly called a shaman. There are few *Dongbas* left among the Naxi. They are brilliant keepers of language and knowledge. I was lucky to have gotten to know one. The Dongba I knew had a picture of Anna Marie on his desk and I recognized her from that. She was dressed in white, flowing robes. Her hair hung loose around her face and she wore a beautiful floral wreath on her head and at least a dozen polished shell necklaces around her neck. She came close, kissed both my cheeks, thanked me for coming and said we'd meet in a day or so. "Rest now," she said. "Our work will wait until you are strong."

She stepped back into the group again and smiled broadly.

The greeting delighted me.

"Maeva" people said to me repeatedly as the scent of their garlands wafted over me. I was jubilant. The attention was thrilling. I know that when I feel myself smiling spontaneously, without artifice, that I am really happy. People couldn't have been more beautiful and wholly appealing.

After a lot of cheek kissing, the woman with the tattoos grabbed my luggage and hauled it out to a hefty Toyota 4x4 pickup truck. She loaded it in the back and told me to get in. I had to hold a handle high up above the passenger seat to hoist myself up into the tall cab. The slim man squeezed in to the seat next to me, and the big woman got behind the wheel. Then, we were off to Besoin, the island's central town and market, and the house that would be my headquarters.

Though both of my companions looked straight ahead and not at me, I decided they hadn't become unfriendly but simply didn't know much English. And, as I said, I didn't know French or Tahitian. It was not exactly awkward being with them in silence. It was just too hard for any of us to string a sentence together.

We finally ventured a few polite, partial sentences. I managed to gather that the woman's name was Hjordis Gumundsdottier and the man was called Jean-Louis. He was my landlord and a sweet, handsome young man. Jean-Louis owned a small Fiat, and he told me that he thought it would not hold my luggage, so he had hired Hjordis, who owned the local taxi business, to meet me with him. Hjordis said that she ran a Brazilian Jujitsu school in a rented shed behind the fire station. How this came to be or if I really had understood her I never found out. We rode on, continuing our journey with few other comments.

• • •

We turned off the main island road and drove slowly down a side lane toward the lagoon. Jean-Louis used a remote to open the gate that led to my rental. Hjordis said something to him and sneered. I think it was a comment on the gate. We pulled up to the two-story, cream-colored, tile-roofed house. Best of all, it came with a canary yellow Fiat.

Jean-Louis pointed at it and said. "Engine okay."

Fine. I understood this perfectly.

"Any problem?" I asked. I spoke slowly and distinctly.

He pointed at the floorboard of the truck. "Be careful. Foot goes through."

He laughed and so did I. Apparently the Fiat had rusted from below and I'd have to take it easy.

"Could hurt shoes," He chuckled as he winked at me. He stopped the truck near the front door of the house.

I'd have to remember to wear something other than flip-flops when I drove, just in case. I imagined the damage I could do to my toes.

Hjordis lit a cigarette got out of the truck, looked weary, but waited patiently while Jean-Louis unloaded my things and showed me around my temporary home. It was roomy and had two balconies that faced west and overlooked the lagoon. It was just a few steps through a gate and to the beach. It had a big kitchen, which

I did not expect to use much, and two large bedrooms, overhead fans, comfy rattan framed couches, and a shuffleboard court surrounded by a raked sand yard. In spite of the burglar bars on every window, I loved it. I wondered, given the open windows and doors of every other house we'd passed, if Jean-Louis was paranoid and that Hjordis' sneer was a comment on overly cautious gates and bars.

However, Jean-Louis, who seemed well balanced and amiable even if paranoid, did not prepare for disaster with no reason. Of that I was certain. I wondered if he had some Chinese ancestry. There had been Chinese merchants from Yunnan on the island in 19th century trading days. Chinese from the south are notorious for locking and guarding their homes. That gate was there for some good reason.

As if reading my mind, he told me that the island had a very small population, about five thousand people, and rarely did anything bad ever happen. Then he pointed at the gate and the fences.

"When something happen, all know and all bad," he said.

"One time, someone steal TV. Someone take bicycle." So he had decided to put up gates and burglar bars.

"When something happen, everyone know," he repeated. And maybe? "Cannot say." It might happen again. It is now, once having happened, within the realm of possibility

That's why they called me. Bad things had happened. Something no one could explain. And everything was now within the realm of possibility.

CHAPTER II

Chien Perdu

It is a good thing to begin with...a mishap...because it develops the fatalism necessary to ...enjoyment...
In Morocco by Edith Wharton

I had an appointment with Anna Marie, the leader of the group that had called me, day after tomorrow. I decided to take some time seeing the village and exploring on my own before jet lag reeled me into bed.

As I strolled around Besoin alone, just getting my bearings, I saw two different, slightly alarming, notices in store windows. One was about a missing tourist. The other was about a missing dog. The official story, I found out later, was that the tourist had left the island and that was that. But the dog...well, the dog was a different story.

There were pictures of it everywhere. The dog was, if the fuzzy digital print of its likeness was in any way accurate, a shorthaired, black, mother dog that had recently given birth. Her teats were dark and hung low. She had short, curled, flag ears and a snarled grin—more a grimace than a smile. Still, there was something almost human in that smile, as well as in her eyes and the way the nose was set on her face.

There was nothing most North Americans would find cute about this dog. Mammals displaying evidence of their basic life functions weren't often displayed in photographs there, nor did people usually snap photographs of nursing dogs. Most places someone would complain if a woman nursed a baby in public! No, North Americans like their meat wrapped in plastic and their females covered up, except in porn magazines. North Americans—well, many people everywhere with the wherewithal to feed and care for kennel club dogs—like their pets neutered or spayed and groomed. They like tidy pets that can manage hours of apartment living or be content with suburban lawns. They like the kind of dog you can walk in a park and pick up after with a little plastic bag in one hand and a scooper in the other. They like the kind you can pull up alongside another similarly well-behaved animal on a leash and let them have a *festif de reniflement,* or sniff fest. The dog on the poster was decidedly not one of those polished canines. You couldn't take this dog anywhere around where I live and expect to be congratulated for having it. It was surely valued by somebody, however, because someone was advertising for it.

The dog was last seen, the posters said, in the vicinity of the *saint de femme robuste.* That made some sense, I supposed. Maybe my ability to read French, if not speak it or understand it, was not as good as I imagined. I figured maybe there was a church named after a holy, robust woman, but it made more sense when I found out from Jean-Louis that "heavy" or "fat" or "robust" woman was the name of a jungled, hilly part of the island, one easy to spot from the sea but not easy to get to from the land. The *saint de femme robuste* was sacred territory, known to be inhabited by ghosts and spirits. It was a place to which one made a pilgrimage if one wished for a baby or needed help. It was covered with vines and tall palms and pines and underbrush of every variety. There were no trails to the peaks, and it was cracked and creased with many crevasses and slopes that some said were dangerous and impassable. What a mother dog would be doing in the area was a mystery in itself.

I later learned that the whole island was inhabited by the ghosts of thousand-year-old people who came here, built rock cairns, carved the stone age equivalent of their initials into rocks, then moved on to the east in gigantic outriggers, steering their way with elaborate shell and stick maps and letting old men find the currents by the sway of their naked, unrestrained balls. Some said it was the spirits of *saint de femme robuste* who kept the metaphorical "heavy," as in the tragic or too serious, away from other parts of the island. But whether or not that was true, the people themselves sure kept themselves away from what was called *femme robuste* for short, unless they were ritually prepared for a potentially hazardous, even fatal, journey. The islanders kept the tourists from going up there, too. Visitors could buy chatty luncheon trips and fun excursions with locals to just about any other part of the territory, but no dice going up into femme *robuste's* domain. That was purely spirit territory.

The *femme robuste* was only one of several areas in this area of the Pacific that were considered off limits. There were several small islands within a three or four day paddle from Moa Nui that had big, symbolic Xs drawn through them. Those Xs were not there because of the spiritual power invested in them. They were just plain scary places. In fact, people stayed pretty close to home since the nuclear tests in the Pacific in the 1950s.

CHAPTER III

The Dog with the Black Mask

*...and a dreadful thing from the cliff did spring,
and its wild bark thrill'd around,
His eyes had the glow of the fires below,
'twas the form of the spectre hound...*
Old Norfolk Saying

I woke up at about three a.m., but my body said it was six or even seven. There had been a brief, sudden, but energetic rain at about two thirty, and it woke me from a sound sleep. No thunder, no ratatat. Just the sound of a thousand monkeys jumping for joy on the corrugated tin roof and then bouncing around on the solar panels before draining down the gutter pipes. It lasted maybe five minutes, emptying all of one stupendous cloud of its moisture, I supposed.

The clouds dominated the sky-scapes that time of year. I had watched them for a couple of hours before retiring the night before. Long lines of them rose in fantastic shapes as far across the ocean as one can see. They each competed with the others for attention—one imitating a rabbit with long ears, another a clown with a top knot, and another a praying Buddha. Small slices of rainbow appeared here and there tucked into the folds of seductive, bosomy thunderheads.

Thinking about the clouds and the rain, I drifted back to sleep until fourish.

Even then, I stayed in bed for a while, eyes closed, letting thoughts drift in and out of my mind. I suddenly realized I'd had a dream in which I had seen that dog from the poster. In the dream, the dog came toward me, blinking its uncanny, person-like eyes with one eyebrow raised quizzically. It was limping slightly and coming from the direction of a point where two paths crossed. Behind and above the crossroad was the crater of a volcano with lava and ash spewing forth. The dog walked right up to my face and stood before me, nose to nose. I heard a voice say, "This is your destination." Then the dream image showed me a close up of the volcano crater. The dog began to whimper, and then let out a ferocious howl. That's when I awoke. Was she a guide? Was she bringing a message? Was she an animal sent to protect me?

I waited until light broke then got ready to go to the market in Besoin. I didn't need the car, because Besoin was just a little over half mile down the beach. By the time I arrived, it was already bustling, if you could call the gentle, languorous movements people made "bustling." Merchants were setting up tables for their produce. Women had bunches of bananas—at least three kinds—papayas, avocados, tomatoes, cukes, and cabbages bigger than a bear's head. Men walked or cycled through the streets carrying plastic bags of bakery-fresh baguettes. I could smell the fruit, the fresh bread, and the salt in the air. I could even taste the salt from the sea on my lips. A monger began hanging long strings of lagoon fish from a tree. These were fish I couldn't imagine eating.

It was as if someone's aquarium pets had been put out for consumption. They were luminous yellows, oranges, and blues. They just didn't look right dead.

It was shortly past Chinese New Year, so there were still big red lanterns here and there and strings of red crackers for sale in the town's only "supermarket." The store seemed to have everything one could ever want: European wines and cheeses, hardware, towels, shoes, fish line, and personal items you'd find in a drugstore in the "States." Cargo ships that came to the island regularly stocked it regularly. If something sold out, customers had to wait for the next boat.

I continued my walk, trying to notice everything. I saw a few tourists sipping their first coffee of the morning and munching buttered toast before heading out to surf or tour the lagoon in hired outriggers.

Several dogs walked lazily here and there. One pointedly came up to my side. He touched my hand with his wet nose and looked at me for a long moment. I'd never seen a dog like this one. He had a mostly white body with some black mottling. He was a sturdy, grounded, well-muscled creature. His head was blocky and his jaw was white. However, his eyes were peering at me from the middle of unusual markings. The black hairs around these eyes formed a perfectly symmetrical mask. It wasn't a small mask. It enveloped the eyes and extended over the skull and back to the ears. The black mask made the eyes, in contrast to it, look light. They nearly beamed in the early sun.

He had a thick, red, leather collar. From its clasp, a tag hung. There was an inscription: Phad. It was written in bold italics. On the opposite side of the tag, the name was etched in Sanskrit. I said, "Good morning Phad" and went on my way. I felt better about my dream. It was as if the lost dog from the *femme robuste* had made a more agreeable manifestation. I thought I'd see Phad again, but I couldn't have imagined the circumstances.

There was a light breeze in the air, and a few fishing boats and a couple of sailboats were anchored in the lagoon. Everything seemed peaceful and just right. Except that it wasn't. There were murmurs, sideways glances, and awkward silences among islanders at times and places one might expect conversation.

Upsetting things had been happening, which was why I'd been called. The previous month, Anna Marie had sent me a thick packet filled with lengthy descriptions of the island's troubling events. I'd read them through before taking the assignment. I'd review them again that evening to prepare for my meeting with her.

According to what she'd sent, the initial mystery had to do with clothing. First one and then another household found clothing taken from cupboards and thrown on bedroom floors. Neat householders were dismayed. Their sense of order was challenged by these manifestations. Nothing was missing and nothing was damaged. Most unsettling was that these items from personal wardrobes were arranged in long lines across their floors. They were not simply randomly scattered about. Most people had very light tile floors, all carefully swept daily and polished by hand. They had to be, because sand was so easily brought in on bare feet or blown through windows or open doors. The bright clothing set out in lines on these floors looked like some intentional art installation.

After the few early reports, the local police went to the market and bought some tablets of graph paper and a couple of Sharpie pens. They began drawing plans of the bedrooms, noting east/west and north/south directions. Using each square on the graph paper to represent a tile, they noted the relative position of the clothing found on the floor. After fifteen or so incidents, it was clear that the lines were really arrows, and the arrows all pointed to the *femme robuste*. There were no explanations. Nobody was seen entering homes. Nobody was even suspected. And it was still happening at the rate of about one new arrow a week when I arrived.

The next thing that happened was the run on feminine products. The supermarket ran out of tampons and pads one day. The cargo ship wasn't due for a couple more days. Things like this sometimes happened. The women would get by. But then, almost every woman who came in to the store in the following two days asked for them—every single woman over about fifteen years of age up to about fifty. That still wasn't all that strange, some thought, until the aunties started coming in and asking for them too. These were aunties and grandmothers who hadn't bled in years.

Local environmentalists had a new cause. It wasn't enough that the coral was dying and there was mercury in the tuna. And Goddess knows what is still in the water from the nuclear tests. Now some "thing," they reckoned, was floating in on the tides from the United States or Japan or even Hawaii that was upsetting the hormones of local women. They had heard about all the estrogen in rivers around Cleveland or Chicago. Was it in the Pacific now? Big tides of estrogen? Or was it Viagra? That could be it, they reasoned. One grandmother started organizing teas: Grandmothers Against Estrogen and Viagra Polluted Waters. They had a couple of marches on the local constabulary and then marched around the village pharmacy with signs one afternoon. There weren't many places to picket, and no one knew whom to blame. One grandmother did a workshop and taught women how to make soft, organic, cotton, washable pads. Another showed how to cut up sponges, tie strings on the sponge bits, and shove them up the vagina to catch and absorb the flow. The market just couldn't keep enough supplies on hand, because there were now hundreds of women getting their periods for the same week every month.

The next thing that happened was the plague of the spontaneous tattoos. If this had affected men, it would have been a long time before anyone would have noticed. Most of the men had tattoos all over their arms and chests and legs, so one new one would just blend in. But this plague hit the aunties. Ancient women suddenly noticed a strange design, almost but not quite abstract, wrapped around an ankle or an upper arm. Some few even had these designs flowing down the side of the face. It was hard to pin this curious development on pollution, and surely someone creeping in to her bed at night and pricking her with an electric needle would have awakened an auntie. No, these tattoos, this plague, seemed to have a supernatural source.

As I walked through the market that morning, I took sly glances at aunties to see how many I could spot with tattoos. I wanted to interview as many as possible after I'd talked with Anna Marie and arranged for an interpreter. As I picked out things I needed for the house, I took a casual inventory of the shelves where women's sanitary products were stored to see if any new stock had arrived. The store was still running out regularly Anna Marie had written. I saw one lone bag of Poise pushed to the back of the highest shelf. It was in a separate incontinence section of the pharmacy, but I knew from experience that these would do in a pinch, and clearly the women of Moa Nui had long since figured that out. I also read notice boards out side the supermarket. There were still regular meetings of Grandmothers against Pollution, and I made a note of the next gathering, place, and time. I'd want to hear their stories. At the police station, I found a bulletin board devoted to the arrow phenomenon. Rows of Polaroid pictures showed clothing bunched and tucked into intentional patterns. They were all brilliantly colored items and dramatic against gleaming white backgrounds. There was no mistaking that there was forethought and purpose to the lines. And there was no mistaking that the island was the object of some cosmic joke or worse.

CHAPTER IV

Glossolalia

We should have a great fewer disputes in the world if words were taken for what they are, the signs of our ideas only, and not for things themselves.
John Locke

When I got back to my house, I dumped out my string bag on the kitchen counter, put the yogurt and butter and milk in the fridge, and placed the fruit in the sink. I washed all my greens and the fruit in water with just a touch of bleach. I took a big swallow of pineapple juice right out of the carton and then settled down to make some notes. I hadn't learned much but had some places to start

Just as I had taken the cap off my pen and had scrunched a fat pillow behind my back to soften the hard plastic lawn chair I'd taken out to the beach, I heard someone at the back gate. Since I hadn't really met anyone yet and nobody knew I was here except the people who had hired me, I couldn't imagine who it could be.

I pulled my sun hat to the back of my head so I could see better, stuck my feet back into my flip-flops, and trudged up the gentle slope to where the big iron gate blocked the entrance to the little drive. I had been told to keep it closed and locked and I did.

Two shapely, dark-haired women, whom I judged to be in their mid forties, stood behind the bars of the gate. Like all the women I'd seen so far, they had skin I'd gladly spend half my limited fortune to achieve. Their hair looked freshly scrubbed and had been lightly rubbed with coconut oil. I could smell it as the breeze passed through their tresses.

I greeted them with about the only French I dared to say out loud. *Bonjour.*

In response, they opened their mouths to speak. Nothing came out. I stood waiting, thinking my pronunciation had shocked them into silence. I knew it was bad, but I'd never had this reaction.

"Hello. May I help you?" I said slowly. Nothing. They looked at each other in obvious distress. They seemed confused.

One said quietly, "We don't know why we're here."

The other said, "I'm sure we had a purpose when we left our house this morning."

"Oh dear," the first said and rolled her eyes up to the sky, obviously trying to think.

"I have no idea," said the second.

I didn't know whether to laugh or try to help them. I spotted some literature sticking out of a colorful straw purse the taller one had slung over her right arm. I pointed at it. She fished a brochure out and held it up to her face. She was even more puzzled.

"What does it say?" I asked.

"Something. Something I don't know."

"Maybe you are a Jehovah's Witness?" I ventured. It looked like something Watchtower might have produced. I looked at the brochure and, yes, they were church people. They were probably looking for converts.

"I don't know," she said.

"I think we should leave," the second one said.

They both seemed dazed. Sunstrokes? No, surely not. They were clearly from the island. They would know how to handle heat. I watched them walk back down the lane in the direction of the market. Out from behind a bush, Phad darted to join them. He looked back at me. I could have sworn he was grinning. Then he turned tail and trotted behind them.

I was puzzled by this encounter with the mute missionaries. In the next few days, there were stories all over the island of carriers of the gospel struck dumb at the gates of homes. The stories were so similar that I thought perhaps we were all experiencing some mass delusion. But I knew what I had seen...and not heard. It was particularly compelling that this strange affliction was visited on the missionaries. They had never before been silenced.

But all of this was nothing compared to what happened when church people gathered for services the next Sunday.

I had to piece the tale together from interviews I conducted the following week.

I wrote in my field journal:
- story was same all over island
- every congregation same thing....The moment members congregation raised their voices to sing, strange languages
- most never heard languages before....some seaman recognized a little Russian or Romanian or Czech or Latvian.
- elderly women cursing ... understandable tongue. Children lead quickly outside ministers praying over....aunties cackled and swore on... were unabashed in their rantings
- Perhaps did not know what was coming out of their mouths.

Once again, it was the elderly women who had been possessed by something that no one could explain or control.

CHAPTER V

My Job

He called himself "psychically hypersensitive," but the staid folk of the ancient commercial city dismissed him as merely "queer."
H.P. Lovecraft

Years ago I realized I had a gift. It wasn't anything I welcomed, because I knew as soon as I understood it that I'd have a busy life that would involve a lot of travel and wardrobe changes. It would be a life that would require patience, attention to detail, and often living in situations over which I had no control. It would require breathing deeply, thinking before speaking, and listening intentionally to stories that would be fantastic and fabulous and not necessarily true. I would need to do all this in order to help to reduce the mayhem that disturbed ancient spirits let loose on the world when they were offended by idiots. These were the things I had to deal with when I started my professional life as an anthropologist. That was quite a while ago.

But first, a little personal background. I'm thirty-seven, about five foot seven inches tall, and I've got light skin, inherited from my mostly Irish family and nurtured by the cool, dark British Columbian life I led when I was a kid. I didn't have time for sunbathing, and I always wore hats and long sleeves when working outside in the woods with my family. I still do what I can to take care of this fair skin. I'm up against some pretty challenging weather when I'm on the job. My face could have the texture of an 80 year old in another five years if I'm not careful.

We lived in lumber camps for most of my early life. My mother cooked, and my father became a whistle punk after he got too old to be a high climber. They were both smart people who read a lot when not working. My mother read Encyclopedia Britannica from

A to Z during her lifetime. Her family were so devoted to education that they had shipped their encyclopedias in large trunks when they left Ireland during the potato famine. Then they transported them by horse and ox carts when they moved across Canada to British Columbia in the 1880s.

Both my parents saved so that I could go for a university degree. I learned to enjoy kayaking and hiking and sailing once I went to college and still do all the above when I get a chance.

I've got short-cropped, nicely layered, reddish hair, which I spice up with a bit of orange streaks when I'm not working. I tone down everything when I'm on a job. I've got a full set of white teeth and a very winning smile that I flash, sometimes inappropriately, at just about everyone I meet. People tell me I am much too happy. My eyes are deep brown, and I have nearly perfect eyebrows. I mention that because most women comment on them. Oh, my name. I always forget to tell people. My friends and family call me Kelly, I guess because of the Irish background. It is my surname, but it beats the first name my parents gave me: Fiona. Fiona Elizabeth Kelly. I'm just not a Fiona. I suppose if I were a writer it would work. I like just plain Kelly.

During my first long period of fieldwork, in my early twenties, I lived in a village on the island of Borneo. My Malay friends, Timah and Gorot, warned me about the Tamil graveyard behind my house. When their own barracks house was destroyed during a King Tide flood, they moved in with me, and their warnings about potential spiritual pollution came fast and furious. The gifts people from the local hill tribe gave me were enchanted, Timah said. I shouldn't keep them in the house. I laughed until the fish traps and baskets I treasured began knocking on walls in the night and moving themselves across the room. Then Timah announced that the window shutters had to be closed every day at twilight to keep the ghosts out. She never missed an evening and made the rounds slamming and latching the louvered frames firmly at around 5:30. They remained closed tightly until about seven in the morning. Even so, spirits began knocking on my bedroom door in the middle of the night. They called out to me, knew my name, pleaded to be let in.

One time Timah and Gorot and I (and their children) made a motor trip up country to Semangang. A huge ball of light crossed the dark road in front of us. We got out of the car to watch it, and it made a lazy U-turn and came back toward us. For a few seconds it hovered right in front of me. Another time I made a trip up into the hills with Bidayuh friends. We visited an abandoned village and thought it would be great sport to enter an old head-house. It was a bad idea. As we examined the skulls hanging from a rafter, a giant hornbill flew over crying out. My friends looked at me, just the way Timah and Goret looked at me after the fireball. The hornbill was crying for me.

I had to admit, finally, that for some reason spirits were popping up wherever I went, and they all wanted to have some kind of conversation. I decided that this might be a calling and that I had better learn how to hold up my end of the tête-à-tête. I changed my field to intuitive anthropology, something I made up. I slowly became known for my ability to connect ancient beliefs and religions with unusual present day inexplicable phenomena. I didn't advertise. That would have attracted crazies. My reputation grew among others who respected the spirits and the power the past can wield over people in the present. I worked alone and got paid expenses and a small stipend for my trouble. Not that it was trouble. I always found my work interesting, and I got to travel all over the world.

I moved south to Washington State after I completed graduate school. The little money I made allowed me to keep up my four hundred square-foot houseboat in Swan Town Marina in Olympia, Washington, and to buy enough food to keep Lucretia happy, fat, and sassy. Yes, Lucretia is feline, if you are wondering. Lucretia is a good buddy. She's eight years old now. She likes walking on a leash and chasing mice. She earns her keep.

I am a loner and like it that way. I do go out with friends now and again. But only with people who don't ask many questions about what I do. I like independent films, *Vagabond Opera*, and *Crooked Still*. I love Yolande Moreau. You can find me at any *Lunasa* concert and any street parade. I really enjoy Lache Cercel and will make trips to Vancouver to hear him. The films and lots of other music I can get in Olympia, and I can walk everywhere from my houseboat. I don't need to maintain an automobile.

When I get a job, my work methods are pretty straightforward. First, I read everything I can find that has ever been written on the place I'm called to, unless it is somewhere I've already worked or done field studies. I start, usually, with George Peter Murdock's *Outline of World Cultures* and the *World Ethnographic Atlas*. Many years ago, Murdock led the effort to code dozens of variables for over a thousand cultures so that people like me could easily reference articles about individual groups or societies. The information was coded and then various snippets relating to one's topic of interest could be located on microfilm via these codes. The *Atlas* made for quick, albeit often misleading, information. Many of the articles coded were written by adventurers, missionaries, and explorers who didn't know what the hell they were seeing.

I found some interesting notes about Moa Nui, things that related to sacred mountains and omen birds and third gender people called *mahu*. There was a whole raft of stuff about heroic canoe journeys and stories of trickster type spirits. I really enjoyed the articles that cited the work of Henrietta Poussiere. Though born in the United States of French immigrant parents, she left New York in her early twenties and became a student of some of the more famous British anthropologists of the 1930s. They sent her to the South Pacific to work among "primitive" people, as they called them. She apparently ended up on Moa Nui for a few years beginning in the late 1930s, and she got stuck there through World War II. She seemed to have returned to the United States around 1946. Maybe later. That whole period of her life seemed a bit mysterious. She received her Ph.D. but the Moa Nui work was never published as a whole. There were a few articles, mostly on aesthetics and kinship.

She was most well known for the longish piece she published in *The American Anthropologist* in 1944 on menstruation and menopause. It was the first of its kind. She had somehow elicited the most exacting details of the cultural practices surrounding women's monthly flow, food avoidances, symbolic representations associated with it, strictures imposed upon menstruating women, and taboos observed.

She was also lauded for a field method she perfected during her time on Moa Nui, one she called, *Intentional Global Ignorance* (IGI). Poussiere claimed that, to call forth the best information, she had purposely misunderstood everything she was told. She continually acted contrary to what she understood to be approved behavior, and she consistently mispronounced every word she learned. In doing so, she claimed, her exasperated informants and others screamed corrections at her. This, she wrote, was the corrective check she used as she edited field notes. Her theory was that if informants yelled at her, it must mean that they truly care about making sure she, "got it right." A whole generation of anthropology students learned IGI and was assigned to go out into unsuspecting neighborhoods in American cities practicing. Many people did not like these students, and some few undergraduates were arrested for harassing citizens or trespassing.

Henrietta's papers were deposited in a rather obscure archive in a small college in the Midwest United States, the site of her last teaching job. No one, to my knowledge, has ever paid them any attention.

Rumors were that Poussiere had married or had a child while on Moa Nui, but there was nothing definitive. Nobody cared enough to investigate. It really made no difference to people in a profession who regularly carried on with multiple affairs and went in and out of marriages as frequently as they changed the foci of their intellectual inquiries. Anthropologists, speaking of Henrietta's Moa Nui days, referred to her as having "gone native." She redeemed herself with IGI and later by doing studies of farm labor camps in the late 1950s and testifying in the United States

Senate for better housing and health protection for rural farm laborers.

So I read Henrietta's stuff. But most important to my work is to just get on the scene. I typically spend a few days listening, looking, and doing ordinary things like shopping. Then, after I get the cultural equivalent of, "the lay of the land," I begin to interview and focus my inquiries.

In Moa Nui, with the foundation of Anna Marie's letters and my background work, I would begin with some serious investigation. I would talk with people who had been most affected by the phenomena. I sketched out some open-ended questions, made some notes on Anna Marie's archives, compared stories she'd collected, and built up, incident by incident, a sense of the whole.

I planned to take lots of pictures and record some of my interviews if people allowed me to. I'd examine the photos and listened to the tapes over and over to see if there were images or voices of people who hadn't been physically present or apparent to me at the time.

No, not ghosts. I'm not one of those people who looks for hauntings. But sometimes you can tell that something isn't being said, that there is a "shadow" present, a perspective not being represented. Also, if you take a series of pictures, sometimes you'll see something that shouldn't have moved. You will find the same thing with sound. If I record an interview and know a television wasn't on in the background but then hear murmuring in the background during the playback, I've got something to work with. I have a few spirit connectors who just love to insert the voice of Richard Simmons into my recordings. Somebody will be telling me a serious tale about something scary that happened to them, and suddenly I'll hear Richard Simmons pontificating. "I want you to get up in the morning and say,' I'm doing this for me.'" Then the spirit or whatever laughs like a mad person as if what it has said is the funniest thing in the history of the world. A few times I've heard Lawrence Welk bubble music. Once the voice of Desi Arnez came through. It's these jokes that have made me fearless in my work. I'm always amused and always eager to see what the old tricksters have in store for me. And yet, funny as they may be, I know that there is always a serious message I'm called to discover or "translate." All that was happening on Moa Nui for example—these strange goings-on—were just the spirits ways of getting people's attention. The real work was in figuring out why.

And I hadn't even a clue yet.

CHAPTER VI

Maps in the Sand

It is not down in any map; true places never are.
Herman Melville

I had another dream in the night. The same dog, the same volcano, but this time Phad came up and stood beside the mother dog. They both began to whimper, and then I heard what seemed to be human voices coming from them. "Manta ray," I thought they said. Once again, I woke from the dream puzzled and wondering why manta ray, that large, dangerous *morador de las profundidades del mar*, was invoked by the dogs. Manta ray? A volcano? What could it mean?

I strolled into Besoin after a quick coffee. Though not oppressive, it was clearly going to be a hotter day. I dawdled over my wardrobe, deciding which color shorts, which color tank tops, and whether to bother with underwear. I ended up with a Halloween theme. Orange shorts, a black, figure-defining Kavu tank, and nothing under. I threw on an antique Hawaiian shirt for the walk. My modest Irish upbringing, layered with periodic visits and extended stays in Islamic countries, called out for more covering. I put on my oft-crushed panama for a little sun protection and grabbed my shopping bag.

The one road that circumnavigates the island was busy with trucks, earthmovers, flatbeds loaded with propane tanks, hand-built passenger buses, garbage lorries, and the occasional bicycle. The market itself was full of delicious smells and sights. There had been no new incidents; it wasn't the week for universal menstrual flow, and missionaries were starting to just stay home rather than continue in their puzzlement. There was really no point in going out and standing numbly at doors. Some were beginning to wonder if there ever had been a point. Islander memory of their almost daily visits was fading fast.

I passed by the bakeries, the shops full of pastries and rolled sandwiches, the plates of *poisson cru* and barbecued chicken with rice. I settled my urge to acquire with a bottle of homemade guava jam and filled my string bag with rambutans, then decided I'd better go home and prepare for my meeting with Anna Marie the next morning.

When I returned from the market with my guava jam and rambutans, I noticed odd little lines in the sand that separated front deck from the beach of the lagoon. They were about an inch in width and maybe only an eighth of an inch deep. They traced shapes that, as I looked more closely, encompassed the whole courtyard. I rushed for my camera. There was something familiar here. Even from ground level it was clear these were not random markings. I ran up the steps to the second floor balcony of the house and looked back down. Sure enough, something or someone had traced a map of Moa Nui and drawn arrows to another island, some distance away. It was as true to the shape of the island as a photo taken from 10,000 feet or so, and I knew if I consulted a chart of the Pacific, I'd find that other island. Incredible. In my haste, I had let my shopping bag dangle over the balcony, and I dropped a rambutan. There it was below, like a bright red eye, smack in the middle of the unnamed, yet unknown, island.

CHAPTER VII

Kilter Line Prophecy and Liberation Astrology

The familiar of "la femme robuste" is a dog. She is a pregnant dog, or one that has recently given birth. The dog and her companion animal deliver messages from the spirits and help women get pregnant and give easy births. That's what we believe.
Anna Marie

The next morning was rainy. I skipped up the steps and out onto the second story deck as soon as I was awake. Sure enough, the maps in the sand had been refreshed during the night. The rambutan eye was still gleaming.

I had a coffee made in the French press with which Jean Louis had supplied me. I ate fruit and yogurt, dressed quickly. I picked up my packet of notes and all of Anna Marie's material and headed for town.

People were quietly chatting, some openly alarmed. A supply boat had run aground, the crewmembers all fast asleep. Another boat had been sent out, so a fresh supply of milk and sanitary napkins were being unloaded onto the quay. Children ran and skipped along the sandy beach just across from the market. A couple of ruddy American tourists were loudly telling everyone on the streets that they were from California. They were exploring the shops that faced the bay, oblivious to the undercurrent of concern. Local women sat behind piles of bananas and called out descriptions of their wares though without the enthusiasm I guessed they might have on a "normal" day. I walked along the main thoroughfare to where I'd been told I'd find Anna Marie.

I found her in her street-facing yard sweeping up dried and fallen palm fronds and making a neat pile by the gate. I knew I had the right house, because a discreet shingle hung just above the gate on a lovely arched trellis upon which bougainvillea grew. The red blooms were plentiful. In fact, there was so much foliage that the shingle was nearly hidden. I pushed a few stems back and read: *Kilter Line Prophecy and Liberation Astrology By Anna Marie.*

I watched her tidying her yard for a few moments. She had a bloom from the vine tucked neatly behind an ear.

Anna Marie was not the only practitioner of Kilter Line Prophecy and Liberation Astrology in the world, but she was the only one on Moa Nui. She was as stunning as I had thought that first day at the airport. Her teeth were perfectly straight and white as pearls. Her skin glowed a bronzy, tawny color with blush highlights. Her eyes were a brilliant light brown. But she had more than physical beauty. She was what spiritual people call numinous: that hard to define sense that the divine is present in a person.

She invited me to come into her house. A row of brilliant red curtains made an entryway. They waved invitingly as the gentle breeze coming from the ocean passed through them from the open doors on the beach side of the dwelling. We slipped through the curtains and turned in and under an arched doorway. Over this door was a golden plaque that read "Palace of Gathered Elegance."

She saw me looking at it and laughed.

"Yes. I stole that from the Forbidden City. The idea, not the plaque itself. Charming don't you think? The whole house is built on principles of *Feng Shui*. That and Christopher Alexander's *Pattern Language*. Do you like it?"

I did indeed like the house. I had never been in a more intentional 1200 square feet. Every inch was the product of careful consideration. The doorways were wide and inviting. The sea was near and at the "front" of the house. The walls were woven rattan and all the uprights and load bearing crossbeams and vegas were painted bright blues and yellows and reds and inscribed with what looked like Mongolian script. One long wall was lined with shelves and on these shelves were hundreds of books. One entire shelf (it was at least fifteen feet long) was devoted to Carl Jung.

As she slumped into a large orange beanbag chair and motioned for me to take another one for myself, she explained that she had contact with most of the local demons and saints. She knew names, histories, and proclivities of all of them. But this series of strange happenings had her stumped. She needed help. And she would, in turn, help me all she could.

"My practice here is my life," she said. "I assist people with all kinds of problems." Reading and interpreting birth signs was only a bread and butter part of her work.

"I'm not a fanatic," she said and passed me a cup of *Puerh* tea. Her *Dongba* friend kept her supplied with regular shipments from Yunnan.

"I'm very eclectic," she said as she handed me a plate of sliced papaya with slivers of lime on the side. "I'll use whatever works and I'll consult whatever spirits don't seem dangerous."

I asked her about her English. It was quite good. As good as mine.

"I studied in Hawaii at the University. I have a degree in abnormal psychology. It was there I met the *Dongba* and the many other practitioners I stay in contact with around the Pacific and in Asia. I have *bomoh* friends in Kelantan and regularly talk with priests in Japan. We all are connected and we all have similar goals. We want a more compassionate, healthy earth. We understand you are with us."

After tea, Anna Marie showed me around her gardens and her workshop.

"This is where I make my flower essences," She said as we crouched low to enter a small shaded greenhouse.

"They are made from local flowers and produced in a green, non-polluting way," she said.

She told me that she recycled all the bottles used in the process and demanded that people return any she gave out for treatments.

Back in the main house, I saw a niche in the wall that had two narrow shelves. On one had a hand lettered card that read, "Place of Forgotten Pasts." On the other was a large deck of Tarot of Marseilles cards. She liked to read cards, she told me, because she had an "uncanny way" of reading client's inner thoughts by the body language they used when she began laying the cards and explaining their meaning. It didn't take many words, guesses, and hunches from Anna Marie, she said, before a client began to fill in the blanks. Those fillers became leads to the next commentary. Anna Marie, therefore, was considered a genius and a mind reader. It didn't matter to me if she used a few tricks. Her intentions were always the best and the results for her clients were always beneficial.

She also consulted her ukulele for some clients. She asked them to pick up one of her many hand carved 8-string ukes and begin strumming. Depending upon the vibrations of the strings, Anna Marie could tell if the client could expect to do well in business, sew a straight hem, hope for a romantic encounter, or bake a successful upside-down cake. If a client felt obliged to begin playing a tune when the instrument was in his or her hand, Anna Marie knew there was trouble ahead. If the client also felt it necessary to sing or otherwise vocalize, Anna Marie quietly closed the session for the day, because clearly a storm was at hand. It would be a big one, and it would come with fierce winds from the west and batter roofs and trees and anyone caught out on the streets.

The more I heard, the more I understood just how all-embracing and freewheeling Anna Marie's practice was. Her "beliefs" were flexible, and she consulted no particular text for guidance. Whatever was at hand would do. I noticed copies of *Jane Eyre*, *Middlemarch*, and several collections of *Rumi* scattered about, dog-eared, and at the ready. Sometimes, she told me, she would open them randomly and read to a client from them. In one session during the following week she allowed me to observe as she read a line from *Middlemarch* to a client: "The terror of being judged sharpens the memory; it sends an inevitable glare over that long-unvisited path which has been habitually recalled only in general phrases." The client claimed to be astonished by the appropriateness of this message to her particular question. She left completely satisfied and, she said, enlightened. Another time I saw Anna Marie read from Rilke's *Letters to a Young Poet*. She told her client, via Rilke, that she needed to "walk inside yourself and meet no one for hours." The woman went home, packed a rucksack, and paddled to an isolated beach. There, she reported later, she found the peace she needed to understand how to deal with her troublesome teenage son.

Elements brought to the island by early Christian missionaries were obvious in Anna Marie's work. During her group sessions, men and women were required to don white robes (like the one Anna Marie was wearing at the airport) and enter into the lagoon barefooted. Those who were bravest or most faithful had to find and pick up a preternatural stonefish and speak to it in its own language. The stonefish, the very fish my ichthyologist friend thought might be the one depicted in the mysterious tattoos, is known as the most dangerous fish in the world. It has thirteen hideous spines along its back. These shoot venom into any creature stupid enough to want to play with it and unlucky enough to step on it. There is, fortunately, an antivenin, and if you don't go treading around on a reef edge, you will likely not encounter one. Being in a trance-like state (Fasting for a week before a session was advised.), most group members managed not to be stung even when they did step on one. Or at least they didn't know they were being stung. Anna Marie acts as translator as the fish and devotees speak to one another. Because I was interested and because the goings on of the past weeks needed some explanation, Anna Marie offered to gather a group the next week (Members could prepare themselves spiritually and abstain from most solid foods, sweets, and alcohol during a seven day period.) and conduct a stonefish reading. I would not be required to go into the water but would be permitted to record everything that happened.

And so we were set. We'd go into the lagoon just in front of Anna Marie's house and under the shadow of the *femme robuste* with the coming full moon high in the sky.

Before I left, I asked her about the dog in the posters. Since it had appeared in my dreams, I thought it might be useful to know any background, but Anna Marie said she didn't know about the posters or a missing dog. How could she have missed it? Anyone who went into any shop would have seen its image. During the next few days, I asked everyone I met about the posters and the dog. Nobody had seen it. When I went back looking for one to tear down and show to Anna Marie, I couldn't find any. I went from store to store and from window to window. They were all gone.

That night, however, I just shrugged it off and tried to keep my thoughts focused on the stonefish and Anna Marie. I went home to charge my digital recorder, take a swim, and drink a few glasses of water. I had negotiated with Anna Marie for a translator. Her name was Deena Serene and she would accompany me on my rounds during the next few days. She spoke English very well, French beautifully, and Tahitian like the native she was. She was the island's only beekeeper and sold honey and beeswax candles two days a week at the market. She was a slender young woman who had a needle-like nose, large dark brown eyes, and very large hands with long fingers. I noticed the fingers especially because I believed she was well equipped to play piano.

"But of course," she said when I asked. "My father was a pianist and I studied with him and at conservatory in Paris when I was much younger."

The difficulty of keeping a piano tuned in this climate had not deterred her in her practice. Though she had played professionally for a few years, she preferred island life and performed only for local charity events.

I enjoyed working with her.

CHAPTER VIII

The Work of An Anthropologist

In spite of Deena's help and my preparation, the interviews during the week hadn't amounted to much. I had to have a translator with me. My Malayo-Polynesian/Tahitian amounts to about five words of what you might expect. "Hello," "thank you," that sort of thing. My French isn't much better. I can read signs and get meaning in context, but I wouldn't be even close to be able to carry out a conversation about menstrual flow or tossed wardrobes.

In addition to the interviews, I took digital photographs of the spontaneous tattoos wherever I saw one. Deena helped negotiate permissions, and I guaranteed anonymity to everyone. My photographs were only of the tattoo itself with enough flesh to identify the body part. I used numbers to match the image to interview notes. I'd destroy everything even before leaving the island. These were only for on site use.

I studied these each evening. Patterns began to emerge. The tattoos were almost all of creatures. They looked like sea creatures. Each image depicted scales of some sort. Spikes sprouted out from all over a central body mass. The "tails" of each came out in a smooth swirl from the back end of the body then split or divided into two, then three then five then eight then thirteen. It was hard to see beyond that, even when I enlarged my photographs with one of my photo programs and zoomed in as close as I could. Even though hard to see, I already knew what number would come next without studying a photograph. These were Fibonacci sequences. That is, the first two numbers are 0 and 1 then each succeeding number, or in this case, each split, was the sum of the previous two numbers.

As I looked more closely, I realized that each tail was a magnificent coil that enveloped the bodies of the creatures. I could see at least three limbs on each, each one knobby and gnarled and each embellished with cruel dagger like claws sprouting from what might be feet. Each tattoo was rendered in shades of grey-blue with just a dot of red for what I supposed to be an eye.

I made a copy or two of one of the tattoos, enlarged and floating all alone on a pure white background. I emailed one to an ichthyologist friend at University of Hawaii, someone who specialized in fishes of the South Pacific. I knew if it could be identified, she would do it. I took a print of one to the dock with me and showed it to fishermen and women on the docks. They looked at the picture, scratched their heads, and said they had never seen a thing like it. Then I emailed copies to some tattoo artists I knew, including one in Hong Kong. Hong Kong has been the source of many fanciful dragon like designs. They've been the rage among seamen there for centuries. I tried to cover all the bases. Somebody must know what this thing is supposed to represent.

When I looked again at my photos and laid them all out next to one another, I realized that each tattoo was really of the same creature but from different angles. Some seemed to be from below, some head on, and some a view of its rear. Each shape held more information. If I could find the right computer program, I would be able to build a model of the whole.

Then the ichthyologist sent back an email with a photograph of a stonefish.

"If it is any real fish, it would have to be a stonefish," she said. "Perhaps one that is mutated and thus difficult to identify with any certainty."

I called her immediately.

"Yes, it is a fanciful highly imaginative stonefish. But I think it is supposed to be a stonefish," she said sleepily. I had forgotten how late it was where she was. And I'd forgotten the international dateline. She forgave me.

When it was early the next morning for her, she emailed scanned photographs to me. She had noted all the points of similarity with my tattoos on a picture of a stonefish. I had no doubts now.

And this was the day of the eve I'd go back to Anna Maria's for the ceremony. I was ready.

CHAPTER IX

Stonefish Speaks

Thanks just the same. I'll have the lobster.
From the journals of Henrietta Poussiere

Whereever stonefish are found, people revere them. Australian Aborigines made amulets of them and hung them around their necks. They made clay models to show children and teach them about the dangers of stepping on them. They are found on and around shallow water coral reefs all over the tropical Pacific. They are very well camouflaged and don't like to be disturbed. Now I knew that this stonefish was the subject of the many spontaneous, fanciful tattoos I'd studied. I knew that this was the fish we'd be consulting later in the evening.

I spent the rest of my day going over notes and revisiting a couple of women with whom I'd already spoken. I decided it wouldn't be a bad idea to take some life histories. Deena came to my place around 10 A.M. We had some coffee and baguette with cheese and fruit. We sat outside on the porch facing the lagoon to eat. I had all my papers spread out on a big glass dining table and we looked over them together while we sipped and munched. Hermit crabs had gone to their nests after making a fresh map in the night. A few lizards skittered on the ceiling of the porch roof. The lagoon was lapping at the shore a few feet away. A few Indian mynah birds darted about in the coconut palms overhead, scolding us for interrupting their pursuits.

Deena was pleased that I'd made progress on the tattoo image. She didn't seem surprised at what I'd discovered.

We went out for the interviews after our coffees. After three, I was soaked through from the heat and we were both ready for naps. It was in the high 80s Fahrenheit, and even though we were guzzling water regularly, we were both just too warm to continue.

I had a troubled sleep. The tattoos appeared dancing in my dreams. Volcanoes. Dogs. Everything was mixed up. And I woke up sweaty and uncomfortable. I took a quick swim in the lagoon then a long shower.

For dinner, I fixed a thick tuna steak grilled to perfection. The women in the market weren't exaggerating about how fresh and good it would be. I could almost taste it before I got it home. I would give it just a light brush with olive oil and then cook it over hot coals. The island women would have boiled the bejesus out of it.

One of the women I talked with after seeing Anna Marie had told me about an organic farm just up the road. I motored up in that afternoon and bought lettuce and a bundle of long beans. That rounded out my meal. And it was a doozy.

After I ate, I walked back to town to watch a cargo boat unloading at the quay and stopped by a small shop called *Chez Collette's* in the middle of Besoin for a cup of *café au lait*. I had my camera and my recorder. I was ready. The sun was on its way down at 5:00, and by 5:30 it would have disappeared and the full moon would be on its way up in the east.

A woman standing by a cargo ship at the dock had accepted an order of flowers that she would offer for sale on her cart the next morning. I asked to buy a bundle of scarlet Tahitian ginger, enough for a large bouquet, as a gift for Anna Marie, a gesture that was, of course, ridiculous since her garden was bursting with same. Still it was a gesture.

As I headed toward Anna Marie's house, a swarm of mynah birds were swarming toward a favorite night roosting tree. They sounded for all the world like starlings. The mynahs are faithful little characters who mate for life and have a busy and intricate social system. Someone had the bright idea to introduce them years ago to deal with coconut stick insects that were destroying local vegetable gardens. The stick insects themselves were introduced for no particular reason. They were brought under control, thanks to the birds. Now the mynahs themselves were the problem. They were driving all the native birds to the brink.

Deena Serene met me just at the corner before Anna Marie's house. She'd be with me to help out through the evening.

Anna Marie and her friends were waiting on the shore at the front of her house. I said my hellos, deposited my flowers in a large jar near the doorway, and joined them.

They had donned their white robes and wore wreaths of beautiful, bright, fresh flowers on their heads. Anna Marie was testing the readiness of each person there by pinching the souls of their feet. Some of them giggled madly when she touched them. One old lady began chanting and grinning the minute the big toe of her left foot was touched. At least, I thought it was chanting. Anna Marie told me later that the woman had been rhythmically reciting every thing anyone else said. I'd run into this in Malaysia where it was called *lattah*. Anna Maria said, "it is a particular manifestation of devilish behavior that has to be exercised occasionally lest a person become depressed or engage in practices that would bring harm to others." The chanter had one of the mysterious tattoos.

I wondered what practices Anna Marie was referring to and whether I might find some time to interview this woman.

The tests for readiness went on. After they were complete, Anna Marie lifted her arms high and offered a kind of prayer for success and gave each person the option of staying on the beach if he or she didn't feel ready.

"I think I may take you up on that," a burly man said.

"Oh?" Anna Marie looked mildly puzzled and a little peeved.

He was a big fellow named Anui with lots of curly black hair, upper arms the size of tree trunks, calves that could kick a football all the way down the field, and a profusion of tattoos on his body. There was something impish about him.

"I know, I know," he said. He confessed to being weak-willed and having had a very large breakfast of several fried eggs mopped up with an entire yardstick of a baguette. Yes, he would stay on the shore.

"I'll help out. Give me something to do. I'm just no good at this fasting thing."

He was given a lantern and told to watch for any signs of trouble. He was told to keep his shoes on. If he had to come help someone, he would need protection against the spines of the stonefish, because he was unclean and otherwise unprepared. Anna Marie told me he was really a good fellow if a bit pathetic.

If I had to pick someone to be my rescuer, it would be Anui. Just by the look of him, I was certain he could do almost anything in a pinch. I felt a little easier about the whole event when I knew he would be there, watching, waiting, and ready to intervene. I also rather liked his casual relationship to the whole event. Yes he'd help, but he wasn't about to give up his breakfast.

Anna Marie had one more word with the group members before they began their, "free will wade." The full moon had cleared the line of hills behind us and was now hanging over the sacred mountain to the east. It was as brilliant as a spotlight. Clouds above the moon were etched with silver, and *femme robuste* to the north of us was a dark outline. The sea, too, was touched with the moonlight. Each gentle wave and ripple caught bits of it and nudged it along toward shore in long, bright, bands.

"Before we go," Anna Marie said, "remember it is the stonefish we must talk with. You are protected by your will, your thoughts, and your ancestors. But nobody is to talk with a Crown of Thorns. They are here, more than ever before. They will try to interfere. They will try to trick you into a conversation. Ignore them. Don't be drawn in by their praise or threats. They are ravenous and easily angered. Avoid them."

A woman named Emere, a sturdy-looking, fortyish woman with a pipe in her mouth, looked terrified. Anna Marie noticed, and, after a short, private talk, the woman made her way to Anui's side, looking greatly relieved. Emere, whose long hair hung in a thick braid down her back, had eaten a chocolate bar during the day.

"She broke the fast," Anna Marie explained to me. "She is a bit too much of an intellectual for all of this. I think we'd have to call her a skeptic."

Anna Marie was whispering into my ear now, "I think she comes to groups to have coffee and chat with other people. And maybe make a sale."

Emere was an Avon sales lady, the only one on the island, and enjoyed bringing her suitcase of products to show the others when they met. Anna -Marie indulged her

With Anui and Emere stationed on the beach, the others began to step out into the water. They waded at first and then seemed to shuffle deeper toward the reef. I could see all of them clearly, the moon reflected off their white robes. There were occasional rings of phosphorescence, gentle wakes of light adding to the magical quality of the night.

Suddenly, someone cried out. Anna Marie moved toward the voice quickly. She disappeared under neck high water and resurfaced with what looked like a sea monster in her bare hands. She held this thing high over her head as the person beside her began to sing loudly. Even with my limited knowledge of Tahitian, I knew that wasn't what was coming out of her mouth. Deena Serene, who had stayed right by my side, whispered, "It is something old. Only used in ceremony. I don't know it."

It was a guttural language with many stops and slurs. Though it was not a pleasant language, she was singing it as though it were a prayer. She took deep, diaphragmatic breaths and was able to hold notes for at least thirty seconds. After a while she was producing overtones like a Mongolian throat singer. The song had many embellishments and ornaments. When she wasn't doing the overtones, she sounded like the best coloratura soprano I had ever heard. But there was not one syllable Deena Serene nor I could make sense of. I kept the digital recorder on and checked volume levels and battery charge regularly. I didn't want to miss any of this.

Anna Marie listened carefully. She held the woman's left hand with her right while she held the stonefish aloft with her left. The beast didn't move, but its back was horribly spiked with at least a dozen erect horns. They seemed to quiver slightly. As far as I could see, the fish had a barely discernible face. The "face" was embedded in a puffy ball on the end opposite what seemed to be a tail. It had a thick gesture of a lip, heavy-lidded eyes, and an abundance of crusty, whitish-grey bits of lichen or moss instead of skin or scales. As the high voice of the woman became more excited, the fish's tongue began to protrude through the lip, which now became a mouth and a great gaping cavity. The lids began to lift like slatted blinds and huge red eyeballs shone. The tongue extended nearly a foot and featured rows of ragged, bright yellow teeth on both top and bottom. Then came a sound–a hollow, empty sound–from deep somewhere below the water and the earth. It joined the woman's voice, adding a kind of bass beat with its own overtone, first barely audible, then louder and louder. It built with the waves in the water, the phosphorescence, and the moonbeams, all to a crescendo. And then silence. With no warning, there came a rumble of thunder and then great cracks of lightening out of a completely clear and cloudless sky. The fish's eyes glowed brighter and brighter until Anna Marie screamed and tossed it toward the open water.

The group members gathered around her and the woman who had been singing and held them tightly as they led them back to the shore. Anui and Emere entered the water far enough to grab arms and elbows and help everyone up to the sand and then on to firm ground.

We walked up the beach back to Anna Marie's house.

"Please maintain silence," Anna Marie said.

We stepped over the threshold carefully. "Right foot first, please," Anna Marie whispered to me.

One woman went to the hotplate in the kitchen and put water on to boil as people filed in. Anna Marie circled the room and looked at everyone, each still standing and dripping wet, as if determining that each person was safe. The woman in the kitchen brewed tea, got a tray of cups, and passed the pot around. The tea was very sweet and slightly flavored with fresh mint. Anna Marie invited the group to take their tea and be seated. They stooped and kneeled and squatted onto big fluffy floor pillows. These were arranged in a circle. Anna Marie sat in the middle.

She took a heavy cloth off the top of a copper lined basket full of hot stones. These had been prepared, she said, before we went to the beach. She passed two around the circle.

"These will warm your bodies," she said.

They were almost too hot to handle. But we each shifted and tossed them back and forth between our two hands when they came to us. We all, gradually, felt quite enlivened.

Then Anna Marie picked up a clay model of the stonefish that she had grabbed from a shelf when she came into the room. It was sitting, toad like, on the mat covered floor in front of her.

Anna Marie. The stonefish. The circle of followers. It was an odd scene, made magical by light of the moon on the lagoon just out the door. There were cool breezes. Whatever fright there had been a few long moments ago seemed dissipated now. In fact, it seemed, I thought, to be some kind of hysteria-induced illusion that we'd shared.

I sipped more tea, checked my recorder battery, and looked back at Anna Marie. Her head was bobbing up and down, her hair shaking loose all around her head. Her voice was a low growl at first. It was then I realized that Anna Marie was in an altered state and perhaps had been the whole evening. The growl slowly became a series of grunts and then something understandable.

"The fish has spoken," she said. "The fish has given us direction." Her voice was clear but pitched very high. She was almost singing. Her words were a combination of Tahitian and French. Deena Serene struggled to keep up with her:

Movement
Magic
Excitement
I'm the enemy
I won't disappoint you
I will save you
I'm not a second rate queen
We'll put on a show.

Deena Serene translated as well as she could. There was something familiar in these words. Finally, I recognized some of the fish's utterances as lines from *Evita*. This seemed strange. Perhaps it was just a coincidence? But the words were so close to one of the songs. And the tune was clearly from the show.

Yet, though familiar, the words made no sense in the context of the stonefish ceremony. Could Anna Marie be calling forth the spirit of Patti La Pone? This seemed unlikely and I nearly laughed aloud when that thought crossed my mind. I was becoming a little giddy. The tea? Then I worried that perhaps the whole Kilter Line Prophecy and Liberation Astrology movement, at least as practiced by Anna Marie, a giant hoax like noni juice, the much touted cure all? People were gullible, indeed. And probably no one but me in the room would know that this stonefish, this ancient specimen of the species *synanceia horrida* was stealing lines from Broadway musicals? It seemed pretty fishy to me.

Still, I don't like to rush to judgment, and I thought it might be good for me to wait to see what Anna Marie thought these words might mean when she came out of her trance. Emere and Anui had been writing everything down and I'd been making recordings. Deena Serene simply looked puzzled. We all sipped tea and waited.

Gradually, Anna Marie's eyes and cleared. After a moment, she seemed to recognize us all. She looked at the clay model of the fish in her hands and, for the first time in the evening, appeared to be frightened.

CHAPTER X

Some Interesting Facts about Moa Nui

But wait. During my week of interviews and spending time in Besoin, I learned quite a bit about the history of the place. You may not be interested in this and, if not, you may race ahead to the next chapter. But I find local history compelling and I think you'll understand a lot more about the people and the place if you just slow down a bit and attend to a couple of tales about Moa Nui's past.

For example, as we passed through Besoin the very first day of my arrival, I saw a tall stone statue on a sizable plinth overlooking the lagoon. I make it my business to notice such things. I made a mental note to find out about it.

One afternoon, after market and when all was fairly quiet in town, I took the time to go have a close look. It was a monument erected to the memory of a woman. The woman was dressed in a heavy travel outfit from the early part of the 20th century. Her costume was topped with a pith helmet that was held firmly to her head by means of a swaddling around her face and under her chin. The swaddle was carved delicately and meant to represent a gauzy fabric. The helmet made a comfortable roost, and there were two or three birds sitting on it as we passed through town. The whole statue, clearly a likeness of a Caucasian, was covered with years of seabird guano. It made the woman appear to be very white indeed.

I was surprised to see this bigger-than-life-sized statue and went to the little thatched office of the Chamber of Commerce near the quay to see if I could find some documentation that would tell me about it.

A group of tourists from the Paul Gauguin were filing out of the building. The Gauguin is a cruise ship that calls at Moa Nui every few weeks. The tourists were all white and very sunburned. The women wore flashy diamond rings and the men seemed to have shopped at the same Ralph Lauren store for their matching polo shirts. Each male neck was bent with the weight of a camera with an obscenely long lens.

An effusive, zaftig woman in a red and white flowered Hawaiian muumuu stood at the door waving and wishing them a pleasant journey. She was wearing dinner plate sized carved shell earrings that swayed as she moved. Her Chamber of Commerce badge bore the name Magnolia.

When she looked my way in a welcome, I told her who I was and asked if she had any information on the statue." I pointed in its direction.

"Indeed. We have an extensive file. Would you like to have a seat? I'll bring it to you."

Magnolia retrieved a folder from a wicker cabinet. The folder was several inches thick. She placed the folder and a large glass of iced tea on a long table. "Sit right here and take your time."

She couldn't have been nicer.

"We are happy you are here and I'll do what I can
to help out."

Her long red nails tapped the table beside the file as she set it down. "You'll find this story most amusing."

The statue was paid for and erected by Margaret Anderson, a spy for the United States in the 1920s and founder of the Academy for Woman Geographers. The commission had gone to Malvina Hoffman, a sculptor of considerable note. Margaret had met Malvina in Yugoslavia when the latter was working for the Red Cross during World War I and Margaret herself was posing as a Transylvanian coppersmith. They drank quite a lot of *uic* together and became fast friends. Later, Margaret was discovered, disguised as a lame Turkic rug dealer, in Sophia. The Bulgarian police, on a tip, entered a coffee shop that she frequented. She stood in alarm, leaning heavily upon her cane. As she did, a great clanging and clunking noise filled the shop. Upon inspection, it was determined that the clunks came from Margaret herself. She had a number of listening devices and other spy paraphernalia concealed within numerous secret pockets in her abundant robes. Among these hidden possessions were a tiny camera, a bottle of invisible ink, a couple of wigs, a code-deciphering book, and three passports. The cane itself was hollow and secreted a tiny single shot muff gun.

Margaret was promptly arrested and imprisoned without trial by the Bulgarians. Her quarters, needless to say, were dark and dank, and she tired quickly of the beet soup and greens she was served daily. Polenta made rare appearances and was unfortunately often covered in tomato sauce. Margaret loathed tomato sauce. The beer was dreadful. However, she was never beaten or otherwise tortured, and, indeed, she was much appreciated by her guards for her good humor and virtuosity on the mandolin. She was released after eleven months and quickly made a journey to Moa Nui to recover her health. While on Moa Nui, she posed as a French woman named Marie Lesueur and seldom showed her face, preferring to hide it behind heavy veils and to venture out only in the dark. She made many nighttime excursions and was observed, during these outings, to fish with a baited line in the lagoon. She also was reported to have cracked a good many coconuts in the yard of her rented cabin. She wrote, ate fish, and drank an incredible amount of noni juice. She commissioned the statue in her own memory and no one raised an objection when it arrived and was erected by several locally hired tradesmen.

It was much later that islanders figured out that the statue was a commemoration of their long time mystery guest, that Marie Lesueur was the famous Margaret Anderson. Though only five feet six inches in real life, she stood here still on Moa Nui, sturdy and at least slightly remembered, if one could read the bronze plaque through the guano.

I asked Magnolia if there were other stories I should know about.

"You'll want to know about the 'Road to Moa Nui' of course."

"Of course," I said.

She placed another file before me with another clack clack of her nails.

"Almost nobody knows this one," she asserted.

It seems that Moa Nui had a brush, though only a brush and with a very short time, with cinematic fame. One of the *Road to…* films, with Bing Crosby, Bob Hope, and Dorothy Lamour, was to have been filmed on Moa Nui. The year was 1941, and the film would have been difficult to complete since the war in the Pacific had started. However, cast and crew had been assembled and all was in preparation. Unfortunately, Lamour became ill on the set. She was feverish, cranky, and refused to eat. All of these symptoms were entirely out of character. She was found to have been infected with Chagas disease from an insect bite, probably during the shooting of her previous film in the swamps of southern Argentina. She was always at risk for these dangerous bites, because her costumes exposed large portions of flesh. After her disease was diagnosed, the film was put on hold, and *Road to Moa Nui* was never made.

• • •

Magnolia poured more iced tea and fetched yet another file folder.

"This is really a good one. How about a biscuit?"

She brought a plate of Scottish shortbread and a basket with bananas. I could spend the whole rest of the day. I was really having a great time.

This new folder contained the history of the dateline. Remember, it splits Moa Nui in half. That much I already knew. When the first calendrical line was drawn, long before an international commission agreed on a standard one, Moa Nui had a small population and Besoin didn't exist. There were villages and several of them hugged the coastline and a number of farmers had modest plantations on higher ground. Of course, it wasn't until Captain Cook's visit in the 1700s, that people understood that an imaginary line that split their island existed. Nor did they know until about then that Americans existed or even Philipinos or the

Spanish. They gathered from conversations with visiting seamen that all these outsiders had different ideas of what a day is or where and when it ought to begin

They certainly didn't know or care then that their island was cut in half. In those days, nobody had calendars and nobody wore wristwatches. Everything was in harmony with the tides and the sun and the moon and the seasonal cycles and comings and goings of animals and fishes and cyclones.

After Cook and the other Europeans came the missionaries. They really cared about what day it was. They celebrated holidays like Christmas, and they had to know when December 25th was. So the missionaries put the residents of Moa Nui to the task of painting a few thousand or so rocks white. They used Wye levels with compasses, telescopes, theodolytes, chains, and barometers to survey the island and mark out the exact line.

All the new converts to their religions were made to carry the large rocks and place them "just so" as instructed by the missionaries. The missionaries said this was a good thing, like doing penance. They promised that each rock would be counted as a plus against one minus sin. They promised that God was keeping a tally book somewhere, just like the plantation masters.

So people carried the rocks, and were urged to sing hymns as they labored up the side of the steep rocky slopes.

One Tamil started a minor rebellion against this "forced" labor. He had been brought in from South India to work on copra plantations by an Englishman. A few dozen friends and family from the same village, desperate for income, came along. This fellow was a recent convert to Christianity.

In the middle of a particularly hot afternoon, about five days into the task, he dropped his white rock and said he would rather carry a *kavati* for Lord Murugan than hoist boulders for Jesus. He saw no pay off for lugging big rocks and toiling in the sun. And furthermore, he told his friends, he noticed no missionaries were engaged in this task. In fact, he had seen at least one "preacher" indulging in a forbidden alcoholic drink and knew that same self-described holy man had a mistress on a distant *motu*. At least Lord

Murugan promised a boon in this life and asked self-denial only one time a year in preparation for carrying the *kavati* itself. Jesus seemed to want a life that was restricted every day and offered in return only the hope of a vague heavenly home.

The rebellious Tamil said he would take a better present life, thank you. He and several of his kin left the work site and carried on piercing their tongues and skewering the flesh of their abdomens with marlin hooks yearly, on *Tai Pucam*, a festival held when the star *Pucam* is in conjunction with moon of the month of *Tai*. They celebrated until local authorities banned such goings on. It was the same year Moa Nui outlawed male circumcision.

The dateline, however, had been firmly marked and well established. Christmas fell on one date on one side of the line and the next day on the other. It was the same for Easter and every other Christian holiday. That posed problems for extended families and for churches with parishioners from all over the island.

As time went on, outside colonizers developed even larger plantations. They were cultivated on usurped islander property and relied mostly on local laborers. Gradually, nearly all formerly self-sufficient islanders went to work for the plantation. Wage labor replaced almost most other sources of earning a livelihood.

Depending upon which side of the dateline one worked on, members of families were paid on different days. One group's weekends started earlier than others, and shops were often sold out before the second group's weekends began. Fights broke out when relatives visited on the "wrong day." Nobody could keep it straight. Some people moved constantly in order to be on the "right" side. Some moved nearly daily and celebrated everything twice. Besoin, the island's commercial center, was established on the west side of the line. There were stores there that wouldn't cash a check from the east side it was dated a day too early. Nobody was happy in those days. This was just too much because to keep track of.

The plantation system eventually broke down, and islanders bought out the European land holdings or simply appropriated them. Local government officials established a big natural reserve on the east side. What was not part of the reserve was sold off as small lots exclusively for retirees, both local and foreign. When a road was constructed around the island, the white rocks in the way had to be removed. Others, off the road, were covered with dirt and jungle growth. No one cared. Still, once a year, people acknowledged and celebrated the now obscured line, which was unique to them, and had much fun dousing each other with water, conducting public spankings, and otherwise humiliating each other and themselves while performing wild, wonderful dances in honor of King Neptune. This ritual was, of course, not "traditional." It had been learned from WWII U.S. Navy sailors who, while on leave, demonstrated the equator and dateline crossing hazings that they had been subjected to while on board ship.

That afternoon in the Chamber office was well spent.

"All finished?" Magnolia asked?

"Yes. But a question."

"What is it?" She asked.

"Is this all true?"

She winked, scooped up the files, and, on surprising dainty, well groomed toes, took a little hop skip to her desk.

CHAPTER XI

Preparation

To be prepared is half the victory.
Miguel De Cervantes

The morning after the stonefish ceremony, I awoke from a fitful sleep. I couldn't bring myself to put on clothes; it was too hot and sticky. Plus, I had bites all up and down my right leg, and I hated the feeling of cloth against the welts that had risen around the nips. They didn't exactly itch, but they were red and irritated. I had no recollection of being bitten, but something had been at my legs while I stood on the beach the night before. Probably some kind of sand flea. I looked for some anti-itch ointment, slathered it on, and took a half a tab of Benadril. Then I made some coffee and walked around in a kind of stupor. It felt almost like a night after hangover.

It had rained most of the hours since about 2 a.m. and there was a fair wind blowing the palm fronds about. The sand maps had been washed away. A few coconuts had fallen, and several large chunks of dried fronds were scattered around the sand of my courtyard. I started raking and sweeping to the sounds of the of the puppy next door crying and my neighbors rustling around getting coffee and breakfast assembled. They were a relatively quiet bunch of older women. I saw three or four that first day. They all seemed to be readers or maybe writers. One must have been taking ukulele lessons, because occasionally I could hear her practicing chords, strumming, and singing Polynesian sounding songs. She wasn't half bad. Still, I was thankful that she seemed to knock it off fairly early in the evenings. The women were all Caucasian, undoubtedly North American—at least all the ones I'd seen so far. They wore excessively roomy, though colorful, shorts—much too large for their little bodies—and tank tops. They went out snorkeling in the lagoon every afternoon for a half hour or so. I was usually finished with my interviews by then, so I amused myself by watching them paddle about. They each had a pair of reef shoes and were very attentive to each other's safety. Unlike the local women, who rested amiably on their floating noodles and chatted and laughed together in a circle, these women were constantly busy and never seemed to just relax in the water. This was not the case. They were just interested and always in pursuit, I gathered, of knowledge.

When they were back on land they appeared, from my vantage point, to be making drawings of what they'd seen. Sometimes, I heard them searching excitedly through books they had with them for scientific names of the creatures they'd encountered in the lagoon. When satisfied with that task, they continued their other business, which included reading. Each had a lovely shade of white or grey hair and each seemed fairly fit. The white looked great with the tans they were acquiring.

I imagined they had to be retired from their jobs. How else could they be here in the middle of the winter? Yet they were that breed of American women who couldn't really retire. Coming to rest was not on the agenda. I admired them but thought the islanders might have the better idea about how to enjoy life.

I made a note to invite them to dinner sometime. It would be fun to get to know them. However, my guess was that it would be daunting to cook for them. I had a recipe for "Buddha Jumps Over the Wall" that features *beche de mer*, also known as sea cucumber, and about thirty other ingredients including fresh scallops, shiitake mushrooms, cabbage, and winter melon. I knew that dish would either impress, or, if not, would knock out their digestive systems for several days. I knew where to get all the ingredients locally, so it wouldn't be difficult. They seemed very particular and had clearly developed habits and a schedule that probably did not vary much. I might have to figure out some attraction to get them to accept an invite. Maybe I could ask Anna Marie to come down and help me do a special reading or some storytelling: something that they might enjoy and appreciate even if outside their "comfort zone." Plus, who wouldn't appreciate Anna Marie.

I slapped on some insect repellent then carried another coffee out to the beach and sat on the driest patch of sand I could find. Time to get to work. I had my recorder with me and finally got up the courage to listen. I fast-forwarded to Anna Marie's interpretation of the stonefish's utterance last night. I took a slug of coffee, put the ear buds in, and turned the switch to on.

At first I heard nothing.

"Ah no! Shit!" I said out loud. I have the habit of talking myself. It comes from living and working alone. Who and what else would I curse out if not me?

"Shit, shit, fuck," I said. My guess was that I had turned the switch to standby but not all the way to record last night. My heart started racing. Had I lost the whole beach and wading episode too? That would have been on an earlier track. But wait. A sound. A low grumbly sound. The sound of a clock ticking. I hadn't heard that in the house last night. More deep but melodic groaning, very like the low overtones made by a chorus of throat singing Tibetan monks. Then, the sound of....what? Licking or sucking or something… moisture ….definitely a sound. I played with the track switch. I turned up the volume. I was frantic with excitement mingled with fear that I had nothing. Then, words. They were words spoken in a high female voice. But not the words Anna Marie had spoken.

"Anui. Emere. Phad, the messenger from the *femme robuste*. They are your helpers. Go to Mauntaerae Island. Find the path. Go together. But first, the noni juice. Drink. Anui will know. Emere will know. Go together. Find the child of the mother inside you. Let the *marae* guide you. Remember the stonefish. Sing as you climb. But climb you must. Your work is waiting for you."

I played it over and over. I called Deena on her cell and asked her to come listen with me. I was puzzled. Did this mean the ridiculous words from the stonefish should be ignored? Did it mean that Anna Marie's interpretation was useless in solving the various mysteries? Where was this voice coming from? And Phad! Phad was a dog. Or did the voice mean the dream dog and Phad?

Later in the morning, after Deena and I had made duplicates of the recording and a back up file on my computer, I went back to see Anna Marie with the recording and my notes. Deena came with me, of course. She was as eager as I to see what Anna Marie thought. We stopped for a latte and a croissant on the way. No need to rush things.

I put the recorder on a table and bade Anna Marie listen with me. She was still sleepy and had tossed on a red halter top and matching shorts when we arrived. She made a quick cup of *Puerh* tea and held the porcelain cup gingerly in one hand while she listened, yawning. She slouched into her beanbag chair.

"Hm. Sing. Climb. Take helpers. Seems pretty straight forward to me," She said then got up and began to fry an egg.

"But what is Mauntaerae? Why there?"

"It is just as I suspected," she said. This all has to do with those damn nuclear tests. Something is unsettled there. You know that's where they did some of the tests. And it is volcanic. It's not good if it is ready to blow. Something needs attention and we're getting messages from our protectors. I guess you'll just have to get together an expedition and do something about it." She yawned again. It was as if messages like these were commonplace. I suppose for her they were.

"You know, sister, you need to pay attention to your dreams. I don't have to tell you that." Deena laughed.

I needed to think. I needed to pay attention to my dreams. Nothing need be rushed. And Mauntaerae Island! That's what the dream dogs had been telling me! This must be the island drawn in the sand, the one with the rambutan eye! And the rambutan eye must be showing the location of the volcano!

Anna Marie told me more that day. But not until she had torn a baguette and dipped it into her fried egg. When she'd eaten some bread and the egg, she started slicing fruit. She put out a big colorful plate on which she had arranged generous pieces of pineapple and mango and avocado. On another glistening white platter she placed a large wedge of Brie and a chunk of New Zealand butter. She put the rest of the baguette on a third plate. Then she made some fabulous coffee. She invited me and Deena to sit at wicker table she had covered with a bright red pareo. I could get used to this.

"It is often the case that what I say in trance is just a way of opening a pathway to the spirit world. I don't know why I spoke the words I did last night...the ones you say are from *Evita*. Maybe Peron power seemed right. Maybe I was just listening to a sound track in my mind. But once the pathway is open, then anything can come in and speak. It's like the ouji board. You open the door. You stay focused. Something comes with a message."

"But what is Mauntarae? What is this all about really?" I asked.

"Mauntarae is an island, more than three days paddle away from Moa Nui, where the French and Americans conspired to mount a nuclear test in the 1950s. The island is uninhabitable. It is still contaminated, and the fallout from the tests terrified all the people on our islands for years. Because we used to gather rainwater for all our drinking and cooking water, we feared they were consuming radioactivity caught in the atmosphere. Strange mutant turtles and lizards and crabs came ashore here in Moa Nui, even several years after the blasts. Even though people don't talk about it much anymore and only elders now remembered the stark terror of that period (and the huge protests and attempts by heroic leaders to stop the tests), it is not entirely forgotten.

"Elders can tell you about the night they witnessed the main test. They all went to the beach and looked in the direction of Mauntaerae. At the given time, near midnight, the sky became bright as noonday. Then, in the direction of Mauntaerae, there were flashes of yellow and orange and green and other unnatural colors. Slowly, while the sky was still light, the ominous shape of the mushroom cloud rose. Everyone was silent, though some were quietly sobbing, tears running down their troubled faces. It was as if the innocence of their lives, the final insulting blow from Europe and America, had been stripped away finally. The elders had seen the impact of WWII on their women and traditions, and their grandparents' memories had informed them of French colonizing intrigues, the losses of language and culture and religion to missions and French schools. Then the French Foreign Legionnaires who had come to work on the nuclear installations had taken even more of their dignity, encouraging whoring, facing off their men in the streets and bars of Aheihei, arrogantly claiming their women. Mauntaerae represented all of the horrors of the modern world and the legacy of European and American imperialism."

"And that, dearie, is where you have to go," she said. "It is clear as a bell. The spirits have figured out that something is going on there that needs to be fixed. And you've drawn the short straw. You and Emere, and Anui, and that dog that follows you everywhere."

"I'll need time," I said. Time to digest this all and to talk with Emere and Anui. And to decide what the hell I'd have to do to get to Mauntarae and what I'd have to do when I got there.

"Now, I'm still not awake. Let me have a little time to myself, okay?"

"Okay," I said. I wanted to be alone anyway.

I said adieu for the moment to Deena, too, and went on my way.

I decided I could walk to town and look for the noni juice before doing anything else. I took the beach path and strolled by the usual Moa Nui beach types. Two guys in surfer shorts were listening to a boombox with AC/DC's "You Shook Me All Night Long" playing. There was an island rumor that great white sharks loved AC/DC, so the boys went out every day with their music to see if they could conjure one up. Down the beach a ways, perched on a colorful pareo, was a beautifully dark-skinned, slender woman, her black hair in a flower-festooned bun, playing an eight-string Tahitian ukulele. Next to her was a bosomy blond lying stark naked on a marlin design beach towel with a jug of cheap wine at her head and a pair of very tiny lace panties by her side. You can't make assumptions about these people. The blond will turn out to be a crack auto mechanic and the woman with the uke, an immigration attorney. The guys in the surfer shorts? Well, who knows? They were young yet.

These beachcombers were a stark contrast to the clean-cut Danes anchored off shore in a spiffy sailboat named *Himlens Hund* or Hound of Heaven after Francis Thompson's late 19th century poem by the same name.

They were an exemplar, well-organized nuclear family traveling the world. Two school age kids struggling with French in the local schools accompanied the two adults. Their laundry was out drying from the ropes and masts on Wednesdays, and they made grocery runs to the quay every Friday. You could set your watch by their daily schedules. They all had bright blond, clipped hair and well-scrubbed faces. When you passed them on the path through town it was as if you'd been spritzed by a cool spray of lemony tonic water so refreshed and refreshing they seemed. As I watched, they motored toward Besoin. It was time for the kids' chess lessons.

When I got to the market, I started making inquiries for the noni. I used a mixture of poor French, English with my special accent. (I always hoped that this accent made it seem as if I were speaking something other than English and usually worked no matter where in the world I was.) I threw in three or four words of Tahitian I'd managed to pick up.

Noni's scientific name is *Morinda citrifolia*. It is a knobby, irregularly shaped fruit about the size of a mango that is initially green and turns yellow or almost white when ripe. It is in the coffee family, though the fruit of it is much larger than a coffee bean. It had been hyped all over the world as the answer for everything from diabetes to cancer to bad breath. It sold big and made a few people a lot of money for a year or so. Then the studies were done, the control groups followed, and, turned out, it helped no one. People locally make juice from it just by letting the fruit sit in the sun in a glass jar. As I said, it had been a fad a few years back. Though there is no evidence that it is a curative it doesn't do any harm. It has a lot of carbs and fiber. It has no more vitamin C than an orange, so unless there were none available, I would opt for orange juice. It's less trouble. And I like it.

Still, the voice on the recorder said noni, so I bought a pyramid's worth, which was about twelve fruits, and headed back to the house. One of those sudden salty rainstorms caught me on the path. The newly graded walkway along the beach turned to sodden clay. My sandals sank under my weight and made the going slow. By the time I got home, I must have had a half-pound of sticky earth hanging from each foot. I toed the sandals off by the outdoor water spigot, put the fruit down on a nearby table, and washed the mud away from my feet and the shoes.

Then I heard music. I had forgotten it was Sunday, and what I heard was the sound of voices from the nearby Catholic Church. It had been a week since the outbreak of glossolalia and things sounded as if they were back to normal. Voices were raised in beautiful harmonies, and all in the Tahitian language. I switched on my recorder:

A tamau a tatou paatoa i te himene i te here
A tamau a tatou paatoa i te himene a tamaua.
Ho mai na to rima, amui to tatou reo no te himene
I te here o to tatou Atua
Toro mai na to rima, ia hoe to tatou haere'a
No te himene I te here, a tamaua

Deena translated for me later: "Let's sing a hymn of love…keep singing a hymn of love…all together in one voice" Beautiful.

I put on clean shoes and walked as quickly as I could along the road to find the right path to the church. I entered quietly, on tiptoe, from the back. The chapel was a lovely, new-looking structure with tiny Stations of the Cross hanging along both interior walls. There were delicate, encaustic paintings rendered on sheets of 12 × 14 copper. The priests and acolytes were dressed in white cassocks with just a hint that these were liturgical vestments. I could see now that the music director had cued up a drum box to accompany the singers. He was a young man, slender, with a sweet smile on his face. Many singers were standing just in front of him, most of them women and many dressed in white. Others in the congregation had song sheets and joined in. The priest at the altar, with short grey hair and a benign face, looked straight at me when I entered. There was something in his direct gaze that told me that this song, this call to enter I had felt, was a special blessing for us all as we prepared for our journey even though I didn't understand the words at the time. It almost seemed as if the priest could foresee our struggles. I would have to tell the others about this moment. I was sure they would recognize the song if I could hum it. I was sure that they could tell me what it meant as I scribbled words on the back of an order of service. But for now it was just something to hear, to enjoy, and to acknowledge for its sweetness and power.

I stayed until the service was over and touched the priests hand on the way out.

The priest looked into my eyes again and said, "Mauntaerae. You must go."

"But how......" I sputtered.

The priest looked away quickly and then turned and greeted me again as if he had never seen me before in his life.

I was astonished. Another message. I felt touched by the music and the wonderful kiss of peace greetings during the service. It is a lovely and loving gesture that seems to be practiced now by Catholics around the world. And now this personal directive from the priest.

After church, the women, flashy in their straw hats and colorful dresses, promenaded en masse to the market to buy ready-made poisson cru, pork, grated coconut, and curried crab. Nobody would cook today. But everyone would feast: a Sunday communion in the truest sense of the word.

CHAPTER XII

Anui

The journey is the reward
Chinese Proverb

I decided that the locals had the right idea, so I followed the Church women to the market and stopped at one of the *roullotes*, local food wagons made from a converted Peugeot vans. The backs flip up and windows are cut into the side so vendors can hand out food and take in money. I ordered a plate of pork and rice. I could relax and enjoy the food. There was no hurry. The initial fear and panic about the odd things that had been happening on the island had passed. People had seen worse: the invasion of the French bent on conducting nuclear tests on Mauntaerae not so far away; the invasion of the French Foreign Legionnaires brought to build the installations for the nuclear tests; the invasion of missionaries bent on converting every single islander. What are a few tattoos, mystery clothing, and synchronized menstrual periods? Not much, considering. Still, the fish had spoken, and so had someone or something in my recorder. I sat on a bench munching and looking out at the lagoon and thought.

Just as I was finishing my lunch, I saw Anui. He was wearing a tank top and a blousy pair of shorts. He was riding what appeared to be a very old, sky-blue Vespa. As I got closer, I could see it was a Vespa 150, dating from about 1958. It had some dandy, still-shiny aluminum trim and a chrome-plated rear light. If I'm not mistaken, this little scooter was introduced at the 1960 Olympic Games. I wanted to hear the history of it and how the heck it came to be in the possession of Anui on this relatively out of the way island. But we had other things to talk about.

I knew from the night before that his English was okay. Enough so that I was willing to give a conversation a try. I really had to if we were going to work together.

After some greetings and the obligatory cheek-touching smooch gestures, I asked him if he'd like to go over to a *Chez Guillot's*, a local pub, and have a *Hinamoko* beer with me. *Hinamoko* is practically the official state drink of the Aho Island chain. It's been brewed near Aheihei since about 1955. The picture of the vahine on it seems a little dated, but the beer is damn good. You see bottles of *Hinamoko* everywhere, even in the hands of lagoon-floating aunties, flowers in their hair and lovely hibiscus print pareo or sarong wrapped around their bodies. I had already learned to like my Hinamoko ice cold with a heavy dose of freshly squeezed lime juice.

I wanted to know more about Anui before I asked him to be my guide and companion on what was certain to be a spiritually dangerous, if not physically arduous, trip. I knew he was in good shape, and I thought I was, but I might need to rely on him in more than one way. We had to be okay with each other and willing to make the sacrifices.

It turned out he was a son of a second wife of a very important man. His original name, Hiro, meant "trickster." He was named for an ancient, legendary person who was artful in every way and considered a guiding spirit of thieves. He had changed his name when he began to believe this "Hiro" identity had imbued him with an energy that he could not control and that was not serving him well.

Anui hadn't always lived on Moa Nui. He had been sent to school in Tahiti to live with his brothers. He wasn't old enough to enter the school yet, but he was quick and listened from outside the thatched mat walls of the classrooms. Then he climbed the ridgepole of the building and heard even more. By the time he was admitted to first grade, he could already read and write and count and name all the locations of all the islands and even understood, and could recite, complicated, important, political histories of the region. He knew about DeGaulle and World War II and Pouvanaa. He knew how to count in francs and shillings. He knew how far to the moon and how eclipses come to be and what the Venus cycles are all about. He knew how to navigate by wind and currents and stars. In fact, he knew everything worth knowing in his world. And he grew to be bigger than all the other youths.

Soon school was over, and his family said it was time for him to take some responsibility and raise a family. This did not appeal to him. He was a strong, excitable young man. He liked his motor scooter. (He got the Vespa when he was a teen.) He liked canoe racing, and he liked to flirt. Though he was encouraged to marry by his family, especially his grandfather, he fell into some very bad habits while still in Tahiti. He stayed out late and made rounds of bars with a group of roughnecks. He even started a band. It was called Bristling Boar Soup and the Rolling Peas. He was the Bristling Boar, and the noise he and his friends made was harsh. Soon there were no more gigs. The band was just too brittle, and their music certainly was not danceable. He engaged in a few petty crimes with the same gang of fellows. He was never arrested, so he had no record. He tried to redeem himself in the eyes of his family by providing starts for their struggling little plantation. However, these were acquired by night runs he made to distant plantations where he stole breadfruit and coconuts to plant on his family land in Moa Nui. He shipped his booty home regularly; the family had no idea the little trees were all ill gotten.

Eventually, Anui got bored with his thieving, carousing life and decided to take a long canoe journey. It was just the time when Hawaiians and other Polynesians were reviving the old canoes and making extended trips by ancient means of reckoning. He thought he could do that, and he thought it would be good for his spirit. He prayed and worked for months to hew a canoe out of a solid log harvested from a tree in the mountains. He used a stone, rather than iron, adze. The canoe was formed from planks sewn together, and it was vast enough for a big man, lots of cargo, and an altar. The journey was difficult. Along the way, he was attacked by a swarm of birds, he capsized, and he struggled with weather and with reading currents accurately. He prayed ceaselessly. Eventually, he made it home to Moa Nui.

After that trip, it seemed all his life had changed. He ate well, grew a lovely garden, hunted, and fished with a dip net in the stone fish trap at the far end of a beautiful, partially enclosed lagoon. He trapped eel and collected fruits from the jungle. He had his Vespa shipped to him and found an old man who knew how to restore it. It was returned to a nearly new condition.

Then, one day in the market, he saw a person whom he thought to be the most beautiful woman in the world. Her given name translated as "Runs Deep." He made inquiries and, to his great disappointment, found that she was married. He tried and tried to forget his attraction and began praying for help again, but he saw her nearly every day when he went to Besoin. He could not avoid her.

She had long, dark hair that showed hints of red in the bright sunlight. Her skin was a mellow, caramel brown. She clearly had an alluring, voluptuous body that could not be hidden though she wore loose, flowing, flowered dresses. Her eyes were deep, mossy brown, the lids above them a natural smoky hue. The color of her lips needed no enhancement; it was a perfect mauve. She moved with the grace of a ballet dancer on small, sandaled feet. One ankle had a ringlet upon which were strung two lustrous, black pearls.

Anui felt as if he were squandering his love on an unattainable woman who would never know or return his feelings. He was full of self-reproach. He would not bring shame on himself, he thought, by bowing before this woman. Soon, he found himself in situations with the man he learned was her husband. They were both competitors in canoe races, foot races, and *petanque* tournaments. They nearly ran into each other around the market buying baguettes or vegetables in the morning. He tried steadfastly to be amiable with him, but it was difficult. The fellow was an arrogant show off who seemed reckless in all that he did and heedless of his effect on others. Anui sometimes could not help himself. He egged him on. One day, in preparation for a swimming contest on the ocean side of the island, youngsters were jumping off high rocks. Anui decided to have a go. He took many deep breaths, prayed, and then leaped out to clear the rocks. He made it. In his exultation, he climbed back to the top and dared the other man to try it himself. He suggested that he was less than a full man if he did not. The man, though boastful most of the time, was nervous about this jump. Anui proposed that he was weak and useless if he could not make this easy jump.

"Look," he said. Children are doing it backwards!"

So the man took the jump. Being a bulky man and unpracticed in leaping, he didn't make enough of an arc and hit a rock on the way down. It was clear that his head was badly injured, and then, when the young fellows below quickly pulled him from the water, onlookers could see that he was having difficulty breathing and would not or could not respond to their cries. He could not move his limbs. Ambulances had been nearby to monitor the swimming contest, and he was quickly loaded into the back of one and taken to the island clinic. His neck was broken. He died within forty-eight hours.

Anui waited a decent interval and then courted the widow, who used the name Marie most of the time. She preferred to use her real given name only with intimate friends. Anui felt some guilt about the man's death, but not enough to stop him from wanting to replace him. They were soon married. Anui was not accustomed to domestic life. Even after two children were born, he was irritable and frustrated. He was easily angered and hit both his wife and children. Marie just wouldn't put up with it. He spied on her, listened in on her telephone calls, and followed her around the island on his Vespa when she was visiting women friends.

Finally, she said, "Look, if you want to be with me, we have to get into couples counseling." This was about the time that Anna Marie had finished her psychology degree at University of Hawaii in Honolulu. She was available and worked very hard to help them through their troubled times. Anui never raised a hand to the children or his wife again. He worked very hard to channel his aggressions. He discovered, once again, that the best outlet for him was sailing. His friends helped him build a large sailing canoe with breadfruit floor planks and outriggers and slim *hutu* trees for the masts. They put it on rollers and built it using only old tools, the kind their grandfathers would have used. They had stone adzes, gimlets for boring holes made of shell and coconut, and sennit or cordage for rope made of twisted coconut fibers. They polished the planks and painted the whole craft with red clay and charcoal. They always had a boombox with them as they worked, so they could sing and make the work seem to go quickly. Finally, after they had drilled and laced all the planks, they were ready to caulk the holes with fiber and fill any remaining space with pitch.

The wonderful thing about the work was that all the women and men who worked on the canoe changed in some way. It was as if their lives now had some purpose and their hands and arms had something meaningful to do. The day they rolled the boat to the beach, most of the island's inhabitants came out to watch. The masts were fitted with tightly-woven mats for sails, an enclosed bed of sands and stone was made on the deck for cooking, and large gourds of fresh water were stowed along with fruits and fish and other food. No canned or tinned foods were taken and no other commercially prepared products.

Launching was a very serious business, and, though culturally a pastiche now, it was nonetheless powerful. Leadership was shared among men and women who themselves represented many Pacific traditions and had learned through laborious studies of the testimony of elders. They had been removed from the old ways by boarding schools, years abroad, and parents of mixed cultural and ethnic heritages who didn't know the protocols. Acculturative processes, put in place by the colonial government, had used every mechanism and agency possible to transform this island community into a modern, western-style organization and to leave behind the "myths" and "backward" beliefs and practices of their grandparents. However, many leaders had taken back their cultural authority and created a very seriously considered *bricolage* of behaviors to be observed with respect to canoes.

First, the eldest man and woman present put sea salt into the hands of all of those present on the beach that morning. These all were called to be witnesses. While the eldest woman began to chant a prayer of purification, the witnesses put the salt under their tongues. The woman chanting asked that everyone present chase away all but the most positive thoughts and rid themselves of envy, self-righteousness, and meanness. The eldest man stepped forward and spoke about all the plants that had given themselves for the making of the canoe. He talked about the history of its construction, the love and care that had gone into each step of its making, and the way in which each fiber and shred of wood was appreciated for playing its part in the final product. Some school-aged boys and girls came forward and laid flowers on the *manu ihu* or nose of the canoe. Then another of the elder women stepped out and began calling upon the generations of people who had come before: the crafts people, the navigators, the warriors, and the sailors. These were asked to lend their spirits to this enterprise, to guide, and to give strength to Anui for this adventure that he undertook, not just for himself, but also on behalf of all. Some teenage boys and girls came together to pour a bucket of salt water over the *manu ihu*.

Then, everyone together murmured prayers for Anui, and, as he was pushed into the water and began to paddle, flowers were thrown all around him, into the water, and into the canoe. With that, the ship was launched. And it was massive: sixty-eight and a half feet long, five feet broad, and three and a half feet deep. The floorboards were twelve inches across and one and a half inches thick.

Protocol demanded that Anui, too, make an offering to the sea as he went out into the lagoon. Anui carried the offering and released it as the canoe made a turn toward the east. Then, as ritual required, he turned back to the beach, got out of the canoe, and prayed with the people on the beach. Then he was really off.

Anui's story of his life told me all I needed to know to understand the efficacy of these rituals. He had overcome his own nature and learned self-control. He had dealt with demons and recognized both his vulnerabilities and his flaws. He was miserable still about how he had contributed to Marie's first husband's death and deplored his behavior toward her and his children. He was strong, fearless, skilled, and knew the old ways, or versions of them, in practice, not just theory. He was a pragmatic man who was human enough to have appetites, including occasional cravings for good food and a beer. He would be a fabulous companion on the quest if he would accept my proposal.

I told him what the voice had said. He didn't hesitate. He said he knew what his work was, and he would be ready when I called.

CHAPTER XIII

Gritty Sheets

Why not be oneself? That is the whole secret of a successful appearance. If one is a greyhound, why try to look like a Pekingese?
Dame Edith Sitwell

I don't know why I even try sleeping on sheets when I'm in the tropics. I didn't get a housekeeper with this job, so it was up to me to keep the place clean, make sure there were no crumbs left about to attract ants or rats, wash my dishes, and sweep. I had slept on the sheets now for ten days or more I guess, and they felt like hell. I might as well have been sleeping on sandpaper. I don't know whether the problem was sand or salt or a million mites and bed bugs. I was just miserable.

To top it off, somebody next door got up and turned on lights three or four times in the night. My little house was right up against another little house, so the light came through my open bedroom window. Each time the lights went on, I had just fallen asleep again. I had to have my windows open to catch whatever night breeze there was, but that meant not only light but also the slightest noise carried into my room. If somebody got up to brush teeth in the night, I heard it. It didn't help that the interiors of these modern island houses are full of hard surfaces like high-gloss ceramic tile. Even kitchen and bathroom counters are covered with tile. It is noisy and it creates echoes that bounce around the house and beyond. You can't put a glass down near a sink without the sound being heard in the other house. One late night, my neighbors decided to wash dishes. It sounded like a jack hammer from my bedroom.

Once again, I hadn't thought I was being bitten. But now my legs had raging red bumps all up and down them. My face, even wearing SPF 70 sunblock, was red just from reflected light. I did wear a hat. I did sit under shady palms. It just didn't matter.

It wasn't a terribly hot night, but I felt hungover again in the morning. And itchy. And grumpy. At least I wasn't sneezy and dopey. It was 4:00 A.M. I threw on an old happi coat in case anyone were to peek through my windows. I fixed myself a pot of French press coffee and a bowl of muesli with yogurt. I couldn't find any sharp knives in any of the drawers. My goal was to prepare a pineapple the way I had learned to do it many years ago during my first sojourn to the tropics. That first trip lasted two years, sufficient time to learn to "peel" a pineapple, crack a coconut open, learn to love to eat immature coconut, wear a sarong, like thirty second boiled eggs on top of corned beef fried with scallions, chili sauce, and soyu, and speak Malay. I'd never forgotten any of it or any of the myriad of other things I'd experienced. In fact, if you don't know about my early history and this love affair with Southeast Asia, you'll never understand my foibles, my humor, and my fears.

I was the proverbial unformed lump of clay when I left British Columbia at age nineteen and flew to Borneo, and, while some might simply grow up in the ensuing few years, I became a bonafide eccentric. I had boxes of books delivered to me while I was living out in that Borneo village with Timah and Gorot, so, though I was studying the spirit world through first-hand experience, I was also getting a very narrow and idiosyncratic literary education. I read Agnes Newton Keith's *Land Below the Wind* and *Three Came Home* and Somerset Maugham's *Of Human Bondage*. I was most impressed (being still of impressionable age) by the horrid possibility of ending up attaching myself to inevitable and predictable pain as characterized by the green-tinged prostitute Mildred. I told myself to be on guard against the Mildreds of the world. *The Razor's Edge* did only slightly less damage to my young mind. I read The *Sound and the Fury*, *For Whom the Bell Tolls*, and *The Caine Mutiny*. In my relative isolation, it was easy to enter fully into each story, to identify fully with the protagonists, to imagine myself living out my own dramatic life, and to suspect that it too would have a beginning, middle and end. There I would be, reading by kerosene light, surrounded by jungle, with no distractions at all. I would read in the evenings while Gorot shuffled around in his sarong, smiling, and Timah wrote in *Jawi* script in her journal. I would read while they prayed, or while Gorot killed a chicken, *halal* way, or Timah ground chilis and onions and garlic and lemon grass to make *sambal* paste for our evening meal or roasted peanuts for snacks. I read while the chitchats, tiny mosquito snatching lizards, tittered on the ceilings and the plate-sized spiders frolicked in the shower stall.

But that was a different era.

It was, as I said, 4:00 in the morning. And I was thinking about Malaysia. "Forget it," I told myself. I fussed on, trying to find a knife sharp enough to butcher the pineapple. I locked my IPod on a Bose dock, selected a bluegrass mix, and fixed myself an omelet with cheddar. It was ten minutes before I realized I had a bowl of muesli sitting uneaten. I ate the omelet and the cereal and drank two cups of coffee.

At about 5:20, I called Emere. I knew she'd be awake too. Everybody got up early to beat the heat. I asked if she'd like to meet for lunch in Besoin. I had to reel her in. May as well start today.

CHAPTER XIV

Emere's Story

...The light had the preternatural purity which gives a foretaste of mirage: it was the light in which magic becomes real...
In Morocco, Edith Wharton

Instead of lunch, Emere suggested a sunrise drive to the beach, past the calm lagoon and mangrove swamps to where the breakers smash on fossil coral bedrock. I hurriedly threw on some clothes and packed a thermos of hot, black coffee, a baguette, some Brie, and a jar of guava jam. We would need the car, so I brushed the sand from the seats, put some flowers on the dash to cover the damp, moldy smell of the interior, and took off for Emere's house.

She was ready, of course, since she had been up for a couple of hours. She dashed out, jumped into the passenger seat, and tossed a suitcase-sized bag into the back. Emere wore an Australian oilskin slouch hat, a mostly red pareo, and no shoes. Her hair was loose today instead of in the magnificent braid she wore the night of the stonefish. She had her pipe in her mouth and smoked as we strolled along over acres of coral bits washed up by the night's high tide. The pipe was a beauty. It was an antique meerschaum carved into the shape of a mostly-disrobed woman feeding a parrot. Emere's skin was a deep, bright bronze, though her back was darker, more a russet color. Her teeth were bright white when she smiled, and her eyes were a color called wenge, a grayish-brown with flecks of copper. Two perfectly arched brows accentuated these beautiful eyes.

As we walked, she told me about her child. Her beloved daughter was far away, and she missed her. She was eighteen and had left home with a scholarship to continue her work in nonlinear physics with Alessio Guarino at the University of French Polynesia in

Tahiti. She came to this work after first hearing that there were, in the physical sciences, studies called chaos theory and pattern formation. She mistakenly believed that such disciplines would help her to make sense of her early life with a wholly unconventional mother. Her father was unknown to her and was never spoken of. Emere, she told me that morning, had had a brief, unhappy affair with a visiting tattoo artist from New Caledonia. The excitement lasted exactly one week, after which he told her it had been fun and left for Aohanqua and his next list of customers. The little girl born of this union was gorgeous and precocious. Emere saw no need to encumber her with knowledge of her paternity. There were a string of aunties, women who came, sometimes for months, sometimes for a couple of years, to live with them and help them with their small herd of cattle, their ever present dogs, and their small papaya and pineapple plantation.

The daughter went off to college, and, by the time she realized that chaos theory would, in fact, not help her to understand her life, she was deeply interested in theoretical physics and determined to go as far as she could go in the field. Guarino was so impressed with her application and the several science fair projects she had completed and documented during her high school years that he made her an assistant and helped her get a full-ride scholarship, including room and board.

This was as it must be, because Emere made very little money with the fruits she sold and she no longer dealt in cattle. Her most reliable source of income was the sale of Avon products to her large circle of friends. She was loath to ask women to buy products they didn't want or need, so she specialized in making available things they really wanted. Lipstick was her biggest seller. Especially popular was the "ultra-color-rich" Avon in "Magnified Mauve" and "Kicked Up Coral." Having two or three or more means of making money was the rule on Moa Nui. Anna Marie, for example, had two boarders. One was an utterly broke European student who made it as far as Moa Nui and had no means of returning home, and the other was a surprisingly small, elderly man who collected butterflies for some obscure museum in Finland. Anui's cousin made part of her living embellishing the dashboards of the island's many Fiats. Jean-Louis raised pineapple and guava, and his wife painted and otherwise decorated baguette delivery boxes, which stood next to mailboxes in front of everyone's home.

Emere's favorite place to sell her lipstick was the Snack Shack in the middle of the village. This was a good hangout, central to everything there was to buy on the entire island, and equipped with nice tables and chairs. There was a large bulletin board where people could post notices of events and pictures of items they wanted to sell or trade. There were a couple of small tables just outside, near the entrance, where women could place the small items, including clothing, they were willing to part with for a pittance or a trade. And right next door was the washing machine stall ... always an attraction for island women.

The Snack Shack women had started the island's first and only collective consumption organization. They had heard about the movement on Australian broadcasts and thought it was a great idea. The movement suggested that not everyone had to own everything. In fact, adherents say, it is a waste of money to own all of the same machines and appliances your neighbor owns. Why not buy collectively and share? The Moa Nui organization's first collective purchase was a pair of really good large capacity washers.

Years ago, almost everyone on the island had been taken in by a fast-talking businessman from Taiwan who urged them to purchase washing machines. It seemed to the island women a good labor saving device. However, the machines they had been sold could wash only about three items of clothing at a time and, like a surly dog, had to be kept outside and tied firmly to the side of a building, so violent were their spin cycles. Even strapping really didn't help. Sometimes they snapped their tethers and walked into the sea, still spewing foam and water. Eventually, the cheap plastic with which they were clad broke into dangerous shards that flew randomly in the direction of their owners. Many of these washers had long since been humanely put down. Now collective consumption washers did the job and offered more opportunity for gatherings and eating.

The Snack Shack was the place where Emere's friends knew they could find her most days, usually with a *café au lait* and a *pan au chocolat* on the table just before her. She flipped her Avon case open when asked and made enough sales to pay for groceries and the coffees.

As we walked and talked that morning, a strong wind came from the southeast. It brought a heavy rain that made us run and laugh. It tasted salty on my lips. Emere turned her pipe upside down so the flame wouldn't be put out. As she preceded me down the beach back toward the car, I could see little plumes of smoke flowing behind her, mixed with her hair. We were both wet, and, because we'd left the windows down when we left the car, all the seats were wet as well.

We had a bit of surprise in the back seat. Waiting for us was Phad. His fur was soaked and sandy, and he had drooled all over the rusty floor. Also, he had helped himself to the baguette and cheese I had brought along for our simple picnic.

"Hello, Phad," Emere said, and scratched the masked head. Phad! Emere told me he was named for his owners' favorite Thai noodle dish.

The three of us went back to town and the Snack Shack to get a coffee and croissant and continue our tale telling. Emere had just begun to talk about her karate classes when a group of women came into the shop. They all pulled up chairs around our table. I couldn't understand a word of what was said, but the women eyed me up and down in between bursts of conversation. I assumed Emere was being questioned and my credentials were being reviewed. I didn't mind. One woman became interested in my fish earrings. They are carved from bone and loaded with detail, down to tiny scales. I tried a little French to get into the conversation, but, as you know now, it was even worse than my Malayo-Polynesian. I can't even remember the difference between hot and cold, and in the middle of a sentence I lapse into Spanish or Malay. It didn't matter to anyone. We ate the best croissants I've ever tasted and washed them down with some of the best coffee available in this universe. In the production of exquisite croissants, the French are not surpassed. It was nothing short of miraculous that this little café existed for us all on that day.

Emere ran to the car, through the still pouring rain, and retrieved her Avon case. She sold three tubes of a new color, "Power Hungry Plum," and had some interest in "Choke Cherry." She sold one tube of that as well. Somebody wanted a skin moisturizer, so she took an order. After the women left, Emere said she wanted to pay for the coffees. She was pleased with her sales. She went to the counter, paid, and bought a dark chocolate desert bar. She brought it back to the table, opened it, and broke it into chunks. It was terrific.

She asked me to come over in the evening so we could shoot some old muskets from her collection. I wouldn't say no, and I said I would bring along a bottle of red wine. Phad hung out just outside the shop waiting for us, and he followed me home. He seemed to know I had him on my list of "volunteers." Or was it the baguettes I'd picked up to have on hand for lunch that interested him? He circled around then curled up on a grass mat right on my doorstep. Several mynah birds flew down to bother him, and he snapped languidly a few times, and then seemed to listen to their chatter. They all flew away in a bunch soon after. Phad looked meaningfully at me and then put his head down on the mat again.

CHAPTER XV

Chicken *Fa Fa* and a Mission

The fascination of shooting as a sport depends almost wholly on whether you are at the right or wrong end of the gun.
P.G. Wodehouse

I walked slowly down a long, bleached-white, broken, coral path that lead to Emere's place. Jasmine, red ginger, and ti foliage tickled my calves and my senses as I approached. Emere called to me from alongside the brook that ran from the mountains at one side of her house. She was sitting at streamside with a single strand of fish line wrapped around her right hand and was dangling it into the water below. She was watching the baited string, peering down in to the water, and gently jigging the line to attract fish to her hook. When one began to nibble, she felt it and gave a quick but delicate jerk. While I watched, both of us in silence, she pulled in two small lagoon fish and wrapped them in wet banana leaves. I saw that she had several such packets. She gathered the packets and stood. Then she motioned me to follow her to the house. She brought the packets inside and put them in the freezer compartment of her fridge.

Apart from the earthen tamped floors with coco fiber mats and the delicate lines of her cane and hemp furniture, Emere's living area looked like a military museum. There were dozens of old rifles and muskets and shotguns mounted on the walls. I didn't know the names of any of them, and she rattled them off so fast I couldn't keep up with her.

She excused herself to change from her fishing togs. She came back dressed in a pair of pale cream drawstring pants and a stunning floral top, featuring bright red hibiscus. Her hair hung down her back and fell in great long ringlets along her cheeks and over her ears. She wore a white frangipani flower over one ear.

We had ice-cold Grey Goose martinis with three olives each before she took down a couple of muskets and led me to the back yard.

In this area, well hidden from the road, she had created a moving target for practice. Out of bits of cardboard collected from the supermarket, she had cut and painted many local birds. There were petrels and albatross, red-billed tropicbirds, brown boobies and frigates, heron and egrets, shovelers and kites, and an entire of flock of sooty and black noddy from the tern family. She had painted each with care and hung a dozen or so on a line with clothes pins. One end of the line looped over a metal pulley attached to a tree. The other end, about thirty feet away, was attached to an old washing machine motor. When she put the motor on delicate cycle, the animals moved slowly before us. If she were practicing by herself, she could crank it up to normal or extra spin and practice shooting at flying hordes of birds. I was a beginner, so we stuck to delicate. She had rigged a big screen behind the targets so all the balls could be captured and used again endlessly.

Before we could begin shooting, I had to learn how to load and shoot a musket. Since I couldn't load and shoot a conventional modern weapon, I had no preconceived ideas about what to do. Emere had several items laid out on a bench. There was a powder horn, some paper patches, some loose lead balls, and a ramrod. She explained that she preloaded a set amount of powder and balls and wrapped them in the paper to make loading faster when she was shooting at herds or flocks. She had also an assortment of small tools that looked a lot like pocket knives. Some were for scraping, some for changing the flints, and others I didn't quite understand. The muskets themselves were handsome. They had wooden stocks and barrels, were fitted with sharp bayonets, and the muzzles, butt ends, and other metal fittings all gleamed with bright brass.

I wondered how she'd come to have these weapons. She said two had come down from her ancestors who sided with Pomare II and helped to win the battle of Fell in 1815.

"It was a turbulent time," she said. "Pomare was good in many ways, but his alliances with the missionaries changed us all forever. Could he have done otherwise? Would we have survived at all?" It was a familiar question, not unlike one I'd heard from people all over the world who had assimilated rather than die and wondered if they'd made the right decision.

She took a shot. I tried, and missed. The birds wobbled on.

Another of her muskets came from a woman in her lineage who fought the French in 1846. She showed me a miniature portrait of her painted on ivory and mounted and framed with gold. I was stunned when I saw it later. She looked exactly like Emere. I asked how it came to be made, and Emere said her grandmother had a special friend who was from England. They traveled together all over Europe one summer. The friend commissioned one portrait to keep for herself and another so that the great warrior's family would have her likeness. The grandmother was so strong that she had singlehandedly rolled four boulders down a mountain and thereby dispatched, "a whole platoon of French dragoons," and salvaged their weapons for her own troops. The French were buried with great respect near a place Emere's people considered sacred.

Emere deplored what the colonial powers had done. She took a few more shots.

I took one more, after difficulty getting my load right. I missed again.

"They took away our language," she said. "We couldn't speak it, study it, record it, tell our stories, or say the names of our sacred places. They came for the beauty of our islands, but then they raped them. They brought in mining equipment and tore off the tops of mountains, decimated whole jungles and plantations. They made of our fathers and mothers common laborers, though they were farmers and fishers and knew how to live in balance with the land. They destroyed our political system and the generations of harmony among and between people we had enjoyed. Though, mind you, we had our own battles, tiffs, and tragedies. But they were ours. The colonists brought in tides of soldiers who enticed our women and left our men angry and without wives. They offered jobs that seemed to be answers to now impoverished lives, but when the jobs were gone they left thousands in slums without the means even to return to their home islands and start afresh. They didn't understand us and didn't try. And now we spit on their money and wonder what we have inherited from their nuclear tests in the 1950s and 1960s."

"The nuclear tests. Yes. What a fiasco."

Emere took another series of shots. She hadn't missed yet.

"Promises were made that they would bring absolutely no harm, and yet the immediate effect was increased radioactivity all over the area. People still collected rainwater for drinking water, and it was contaminated. One whole island, the island used to stage the tests, had to be evacuated, abandoned, for the wind had changed at the last minute, and that island was in the path.

We talked on and on while we loaded and fired our muskets. I was not good at this sport. I finally put mine down and just watched and listened.

Emere firmly believed that whatever was going on now on Moa Nui had to do with the nuclear tests. The earth, she thought, had been injured, perhaps irreparably. She would do whatever it took to help. I hadn't told her yet that the message from the stonefish was in full agreement.

I took up my musket again for one more try. This time, I managed to hit a few birds. I think I put a hole through a noddy and an albatross. My excuses, made silently to my wounded ego self, were that these muskets weren't very accurate and they didn't have sights. So really, on my part, it was just hit or miss, willy-nilly. Emere's balls continued to make loud splats as they pierced the cardboard quarry with each shot.

We went into the house for dinner. She pulled the cold fish out of the freezer, dressed them, and grilled them. She served a large casserole of chicken *fa fa*. It is a fabulous stew made of chicken, garlic, coconut milk, onion and spinach. She had topped hers with toasted, shredded coconut. I was in heaven. All my embarrassment over my musket performance fell away. She served a large salad of fruits and greens, all from her garden, all freshly plucked. We had papaya and lime for dessert.

I was taken with Emere. She was the kind of woman who created drama with the placement of a comb in her hair and caused excitement with a pair of earrings. I could imagine that the place behind her ear smelled of frangipani. Her skin was always slightly moist and her bare shoulders looked as if they were sprayed with silk. There was nothing about her that was not alive. And yet, in spite of her softness, she was a fierce, almost archetypal matriarch, leader, and warrior. I was glad she was on my side.

By the end of the evening I told her about Mauntaerae and what we had to do. She was ready. No surprise.

I left for home elated.

CHAPTER XVI

Lest I Forget

*All abstract sciences are nothing but the study
of relations between signs.*
Denis Diderot

It was almost as if the spirits thought I was getting a little too cozy. The next morning all hell broke loose on the island. The first thing I heard in the market was that a sacred penis rock had moved twenty meters east and suddenly looked uncircumcised. I quickly found Deena and we drove to a place where we could see the rock. To my eyes, it looked more like King Kong than a penis. However, there was no mistaking. It really had "traveled." I had some pictures of it from when I'd been on this part of the island before. I clicked back through my camera archives and compared the photo to location that day. It was definitely in a new place. Also it really did have new rocks clustered about it now. People claimed these looked like foreskin. When I got back to the market, many people had brought out photographs from their own collections. There were pictures from a number of vantage points that showed where the rock had been before and how it had looked. There were conversations about the rock everywhere.

But there was more to tell. The few people who still had the plastic washers and who hadn't joined the collective came to town with the news that their plastic washing machines had broken loose from their cords and ropes, "walked" several feet, waded into the lagoon, and then shattered into hundreds of pieces. There was not one plastic washer left whole on the entire island now. Granted, everyone knew they were cheap and the plastic had stressed in the heat and sun. But still, why would the remaining twenty-five or so all make a break for it on the same day? (Later that week, new applications were made to the collective. That was good news for everyone. There would be so many things that could be purchased now.)

As the day wore on, even more people gathered in Besoin and began to tell stories. I noticed Magnolia taking notes. Turns out Magnolia IS the Chamber of Commerce on Moa Nui. And she also puts out a weekly newssheet. She covers all local events. She had her hands full today.

With these latest mysteries, people decided to speak about very unexplained event. Nothing was too farfetched. Someone suggested that they all gather under a large shelter near the quay. There were benches there and some chairs were fetched for the comfort of elders.

People spoke, taking turns, in great detail during this extemporaneous public forum on the quay. Anna Marie came just after speeches began and acted as a sort of moderator. Deena stayed right by me interpreting at break neck speed. As stories were compared, it was discovered that the visor on the driver side of every Fiat had snapped off that morning. Six people had visited local clinics with the complaint that they had fallen off their hammocks. All had sore butts and bruised ankles. Six more aunties had new tattoos. One man had diarrhea, but everyone agreed that was caused by eating too much *mape*, a local steamed chestnut like delicacy. These were some pretty strange messages, but messages they were, and it was clear to me that my work had only just begun. I'd had enough of these lovely conversations with cocktails, muskets, and the charming Emere. The spirits were underscoring the urgency of our mission. We had to get going if we were going to save the day!

CHAPTER XVII

Phad

Whom but a dusk misfeatured messenger, no other than the angel of this life, whose care is lest men see too much at once.
Robert Browning

Phad was not a stray dog. He did, after all, have a collar. He had owners who cared for him as if he were their child. He belonged to Henri and Loretta, who owned a fabulous French restaurant called Le Grand Thon just across from the quay. Henri had learned to cook from his mother, Helene Abarron, a restaurateur in a three star Michelin restaurant just outside of Paris called Le Coeur de Anton.

Helene had a Basque background and cooked surprising dishes from that region of France. She introduced *la plancha* to her many guests with great success. Only a very few early customers managed to burn themselves on her original open fire version. Of those, only one had to be hospitalized. Helene was famous for her carelessness in dress and manners and use of heat sources. She was beloved by all, in part because of her casual approach to service. Even the injured party came knowing of the risks involved at dining at Le Coeur de Anton. Thus she was saved from the embarrassment of a protracted lawsuit. Since the introduction of an electric model, all has gone well, Henri assured me during our conversations. He told me that her *Jambon de Bayonne* is exquisite and served with *Piment d'Espelette*, of course. But aside from Basque specialties, Helene, Henri said, taught him to prepare all the soups and sauces and gratins and *buerre meunieres* he would ever want to serve. He learned how to catch and prepare *anguille*, how to dress with *anchoix*, and how to flavor with *amande*. He learned to make *blanquette* and *boudin* noir. He learned to tie a mean *bouquet garni* and braise a brisket and brown a *brulee*. In short, he knew all that Helene knew.

He met Loretta in the village where his mother's restaurant was located. She was a budding *chanteuse*, a local girl of enormous talent. They married years ago when they were still young. Though happy, Henri and Loretta wanted adventure and became bored with village and restaurant life. Loretta's family clung to her like moss, and the young couple spent their evenings in their little home, against their own wishes, watching a boring television show called something like, *le grand perdant*," on an antique black and white television with Loretta's brothers, sisters, nephews, nieces, aunties and uncles snugged next to them on a too-small faux leather davenport. So they packed up all of Henri's pots and pans and all of Loretta's dancing shoes, net stockings, and musical scores and headed for the South Pacific. They left the television and davenport and sublet the flat to the family.

For a short while, when they were living on one of the more populous and larger islands, Loretta performed on various piers as the big tourist boats landed. She was fabulous. She had many petticoats, a small Tahitian ukulele, and a small Spanish button accordion, and she switched deftly from instrument to instrument and could dance and sing while playing either of them. Unlike many European women, her hips and middle were not inhibited in their movements. She not only kicked but also wiggled. Every part of her could move with lovely precision and to the delight of all onlookers. She preferred dressing in dark reds and black.

Henri, meanwhile, converted a Peugeot van and sold crepes from his griddle to the crowds she drew to her. The act of the superb Loretta pulled in dozens of customers who became so enchanted that they wished to stay. Once they ordered a crepe from Henri, they would decide to have a seat and order even more while listening to Loretta and watching her snagged-stocking-clad legs tapping along the splintered decking of the dock. She varied her act and added new enticements when interest waned. She was able, at the end of this phase of their careers, to tightrope walk diagonally up to the cargo holds of ships that were in port. Then she opened a small parasol and floated down like a bit of dandelion fluff.

After several successful seasons, she invited, for one season, her twin uncles from Romania to come play cimbalons. They brought with them their neighbor, a superb Roma violinist. The act now regularly drew hundreds of followers. The crepes were filled with increasingly exotic fruits and nuts and sauces. One uncle made knishes on Fridays. The Roma made a divine cabbage slaw. The other uncle devised a recipe for mahi mahi sausage, but it did not do well.

Henri and Loretta knew they could make money now. Helene was sent word that the couple would make this new place their home. Helene mourned this decision but wished them the best, of course.

So Henri and Loretta began looking for an island and village that was small and peaceful and where they could open a real restaurant. They found Moa Nui by chance.

Phad (called Boris by them in those days) arrived one day as a small pup. He was left on the doorstep of their Peugeot van, wrapped in a coconut leaf and tucked into a wooden box meant to carry tins of mackerel. They kept him, of course. By the time they had begun looking for a new home, Boris was about a year old. He traveled with them on a large freighter. The ship sailed from island to island with goods and people. Into its cargo hold they had loaded all their possessions.

The couple had no plan. Henri and Loretta simply trusted they'd know when they'd come to the right place. When they pulled into Moa Nui, Boris became very excited and began barking and pacing the deck. When the cargo hold opened and the gang plank was put down, Boris raced into the town. Henri and Loretta had about twenty minutes before the boat would leave again. They followed Boris. He stood stalk still, one paw up and tail stiff and parallel to the ground, pointing at a boarded up restaurant with a sign on it that said "a vendre." For sale. That was that.

I talked a long time with Henri and Loretta about taking Phad on the trip. They understood he had special gifts, and they understood the importance of our mission. I chucked Phad under the chin and scruffed his head. He was on board, whole-heartedly. He would not require much. Just his kibble and fresh water and he'd be set for our journey.

CHAPTER XVIII

The Pits of Despair

Whenever I prepare for a journey I prepare as though for death.
 Katherine Mansfield

Emere, Anui, Phad, and I were making ready for our trip. For Phad, this meant bouncing around excitedly and nipping at our feet when we were all together planning. Sometimes he would grab someone's lunch basket or a garment and run some distance, inviting a play-break. We learned that these breaks were usually welcome and saved our backs and arms from being over-worked.

We had decided we would go in Anui's old canoe. It would be a long journey—at least three days—with unknown challenges. We made lists, visited each other daily, and had dinners together to compare what we wanted to bring so we didn't duplicate items. We were excited by the prospect of the trip itself but also knew there were dangers.

Within a week or so of agreeing to the trip, we helped Anui pull his canoe out of the storage shed it had been in for years. Anui had used *calophyllum inophyllum* (kamani) for the hull and breadfruit for most other wooden parts, so everything was still in very good shape. Some patching and sprucing up was necessary. And, of course, everything had to be checked for strength and endurance at least two times over. We began mixing red clay and coconut oil to paint over the hull, the ribs, the spreaders, and the steering oars. We looked for any sign of weakness or worm holes. We plaited new mats out of pandanus and coconut for sails and replaced all the cordage with a combination of hibiscus and coconut fiber. All this repair work was good practice for working together. We learned songs and chants that would help us both pass the time on the sea and protect us. Our little workshop on the seaside became a favorite hangout for small boys and girls who rafted up to our beach in small fiberglass kayaks or arrived in platoons of old fat tire bicycles to sing and play with us. When they tired of our company, they would jump into the lagoon and carouse like so many dolphins. These kids were incredibly strong and agile and very good-humored.

But even as we made our preparations, there were more signs. A 6.3 earthquake hit New Zealand and practically leveled Christchurch. A fellow called Moon Man said an even larger one would come the next month. He was a mathematician and claimed he could use moon phases, tides, and the closeness of moon to earth (perigee) to predict major upheavals. Apparently all of these calculations had nothing to say about revolutions in the Middle East, the calving of glaciers, and the demise of the polar bear's hunting territory. But Moon Man carried enough weight that New Zealanders were stashing belongings into cars and wagons and moving vans and getting the hell out of Christchurch by the droves. It was a real panic and nothing scientists said on repeated televised broadcasts could allay the fears.

Back home on Moa Nui, the earthquake predictions fueled fear of a major tsunami. Well, fear is putting it strongly. There had been tsunamis before, and people knew what to do. In fact, a modern system of sirens, hooked up with NOAA's Pacific Tsunami Warning Center in Hawaii, had replaced the practice of sending young men up and down beaches hollering and checking each house along the shore. Some island matrons still preferred the young men and had actually looked forward to the spectacle and excitement of watching these handsome fellows do their civic duty, regardless of the danger of the actual tsunami. Many still refused to leave at the sound of the sirens and had to be pulled and lifted to safety by a team of volunteer dandies. One small group of matrons just in the past year had broken into the warning center, hit the button, and scrambled back to their homes to be evacuated. They were, in this instance, dressed and coifed for the occasion. It was a minor scandal, but, as in bingo and other community games, the matriarchs were cut a lot of slack.

The most laid-back of the islanders, who had by now accommodated a whole host of strange happenings, now planned tsunami parties should the new earthquakes generate one. One older, very experienced and brave woman, one of the many island "expats," had invited everyone within a three mile radius of her place to assemble at her home when the warning came for real. Her house was set well back from the beach and its protective lagoon. The plan was to grab all the bottles of booze and mixers in her cabinets, jump the fence that separated her place from the neighbor's pot garden, pull up a few of his plants, and then run up the terraced hillside into the mountains. She figured the whole party could survive for a year up there if it had to.

Meanwhile, and unrelated to the tsunami, a woman from Yap arrived on a cargo ship with unsettling news of a complicated relationship she was escaping. She was a welcome distraction from the worrisome events of the past weeks. Everyone talked about her. She was a lively, shapely person with bright white teeth and strong limbs who was, we suspected, in her early fifties. She would not say.

In her village on Yap, she had met a younger man in a pub one evening. He was handsome and charming, and, though still married, she was willing to leave her old man and move in with this fellow. She hadn't heard the rumors that every woman he had run with seemed to eventually disappear. If she had heard, she probably wouldn't have believed them, so smitten was she by the young man. After a few days and nights of love making, she became ravenous for food. He brought her a platter of land crabs, perhaps the ugliest meal she'd ever been served. He brought the food right to the bed and served them, with a flourish, on a silver tray. The crabs were covered with fine filaments and were grayish-green. One was still alive. None had been cleaned very well. In fact, there was an abundant amount of mud caked to their claws. "Oh well," she thought. "So he is a little on the savage side. So he is not a very good cook. But he is handsome and a great lover."

She could put up with a few flaws, she told herself. The next day, he brought her a golden tray of live frogs and some horrible soft nuts and some fermented coconut milk that had flies floating in it. The next day, when she asked for a glass of water, he brought her a pitcher of macaque urine...which was odd because there were no macaques on Yap, at least none that anyone had ever seen.

The sex was one thing, but this fellow was clearly peculiar. She started packing up her things to leave. The man fell on the floor to block the exit and quickly turned into a very slimy, deep-green lizard. She hopped over him, ran all the way to the town, drew some money from her bank, grabbed her passport, and left. The lizard followed her as far as the tarmac.

The Yap woman wasn't terribly traumatized by all of this nor was she put off men. After her arrival in Moa Nui, she immediately started hanging out in *Chez Guillot's* and picking up other handsome younger fellows. We began to wonder if her story of the lizard man was a fabrication intended to gather attention. I was fairly certain that her issues had nothing to do with our problems and quest.

Except that she could be a major distraction for Anui. Emere and I met with him several times to persuade him not to become involved with her. She had already made a couple of passes at him. Nothing is much is secret on Moa Nui. We reminded him of Marie, his wife. We patrolled *Chez Guillot's* and other pubs in the evenings. We set up a watch outside his door. Phad sat patiently with us without comment.

Finally, happily, the woman boarded an afternoon flight to L.A. We were all relieved.

CHAPTER XIX

More Pits

Rumble of the rock and the walls closed round
The living and the dead men two miles down.
Spring Hill Mine Disaster, Peggy Seeger

During this same period, someone came back from a trip to visit her doctor on an island called Moawea. She visited this doctor periodically for her bad knees and had the oil of emu injected straight into the joints. This seemed to alleviate pain for a week or two at a time, and the only bad effect from the oil was the profusion of hair that grew around the entry point of the needle. It was a downy white fluff and very obvious against her brown legs and otherwise smooth skin. Still, if it eased the agony, why not?

When she returned from this particular trip, however, the news was grim. Several hunters and hikers on an island called Moawea had disappeared up in the mountains. Rescue teams sent to look for them discovered that giant pits had opened all over the hillsides. Authorities discouraged all further hiking. That included disallowing the collection of mountain fruits and vines for manufacturing chairs and other craft items. This was a blow to the local economy. The mayor organized a big force to begin combing the mountains in pairs. Each member of the force had flags and crime tape with which to mark the holes. But the chasms and craters were opening and collapsing on themselves almost faster than they could be marked, and they were thoroughly disguised by the surrounding vegetation. Teams often had to call for help. Ropes were deployed to pull the hapless troopers out of the abysses into which they had fallen. They were sometimes as deep as a hundred feet.

A geologist was flown in from the nearest university and asked to find out what was going on. She plotted the hill sides and location of the pits with her GPS. It didn't take long to realize that the pits were opening over the underground tunnels associated with a long defunct phosphate operation dug and worked for years by the colonial government. The whole island was undermined by worm holes. There was literally nothing to be done about it. The only safe areas were around the ports and the shore. From the air, the island looked as if it had been bombed for the pits were growing to crater size. There was a mood of bitter despair everywhere.

At least there was an explanation for the problems on Moawea.

Back home on Moa Nui, the mysteries continued. A rooster started yelling out "I love you" every morning instead of crowing. A tree full of mynah birds began laughing and sneering every time someone walked nearby. The ocean was blood red one sunrise.

CHAPTER XX

Almost Ready to Go...But...

*If it wasn't for bad luck,
I wouldn't have no luck at all.*
Booker T. Jones

I had planned to take all the personal items I needed for the trip to the canoe and stash them there the day before our departure date. I packed the car, backed up, and pointed the clicker at the electric gate. Nothing happened. I clicked again. Nothing. The house I had been provided with had concrete walls topped with barbed wire all around and that heavy, iron, automatic front gate I noted on the first day when I moved in. There was no way out or in if you couldn't open the gate. I figured it was just a simple malfunction. I turned off the car and started back inside to call the house's owner, Jean-Louis, whom I really hated to bother. I thought all the security was ridiculous. (As, apparently, so did Hjordis.) However, I respected Jean-Louis' rules and kept things locked up tight. I was embarrassed that I might have made some silly mistake or broken the thing. Still, I had to call him.

I put the key in the front door to turn it and nothing happened. I knew it was the correct key in my hand. I tried again. I tried turning it the other way. I took the key out of the lock and stared at it. No, this was the right key. I thought, oh well, let's try the other door. It wouldn't open either. I could not imagine how I had mixed up the keys. I remembered that the upstairs balcony door wasn't locked, so I scaled the filigreed iron door that fit over the wooden kitchen door and hopped onto the balcony. Though there were burglar bars, I was able to squeeze through a wobbly pair and get in the house. I picked up the receiver from the phone to call Jean-Louis, but no dial tone. Nothing worked. All the power was off. I checked the fuse box. Everything looked fine.

Then I thought maybe there was a strike called. The workers in the mayor's office had been upset about wages. Maybe they had closed down the island power plant. I went back outside and scaled the iron gate. I managed to avoid the sharp spikes that were spaced every five or six inches. I let myself down on the other side. Then I walked into town. As it turned out, there was no power on the whole island, and nobody knew why. The airport was shut down because all communications were out. No telephone, no internet, no refrigeration. We just had to wait to see what next.

At the same time, several people from different parts of the island reported that European men had gone missing in addition to the "tourist" who had disappeared before I arrived. The latter mystery had been solved. The fellow had been an entrepreneur who intended to buy up land at the base of the *femme robuste* for an eighteen-hole golf course. Magnolia had tracked the man back to his home country using information from his visa, which was on file with the immigration authorities. She dug up the story and printed it just before the disappearance. His deceit enraged islanders, so it was no real wonder that fellow had "gone missing." More likely, he had hired a boat and gotten the heck away before he could be confronted. He knew not to show his face on Moa Nui again.

Now there were more men gone. Their elegant, expensive homes had been found empty during the past month or so. No one had mentioned it until now because sometimes these men would fly to Tahiti or even Hawaii on short junkets. But it had been several weeks since they were last seen. The stories were all the same. They had built beautiful homes on land acquired through shady deals with the colonial government. They had flown in extravagant building materials—teak and other hardwoods from depleted, presumably protected, forests of Bangkok and Indonesia and Brazil. They had underpaid local labor to build for them. They had not respected the land's value to the people and had clear-cut prime jungle land and desecrated *marae*. Now all of them seemed to be gone. Their cars sat in driveways, meals half-prepared sat on stoves, baguettes had turned to stone, Brie was rotting, and expensive wine gone to vinegar. Their fruit was not harvested, and their clothing and other belongings were undisturbed. Even their passports were found. The men had disappeared and yet had not been booked as passengers on departing ships or airplanes. No one knew what to do. It was decided that if they hadn't returned in six months, the houses would be auctioned off either in whole or in part and the proceeds used to build a gymnasium for the children of the island.

That solution did not, of course, address the issue of the flies. Before I was back in my compound, a cloud that looked like a million locust came in over the mountain top from the southeast. They were a sort of blue bottle fly. They landed in the center of town. Every teenage girl on the island was sent for and given the job of swatting. Very old, ritual swatters were brought out of musty trunks. They were the swatters used by great-great-grandmothers and were very effective. They were whisks really, not swatters. The girls were promised a small stipend, and for the whole rest of the day one could hear nothing but buzz, whack, and whisk coming from the town.

Then the flies were gone and the power came back on. Just like that.

After listening to the gossip, much of which I couldn't understand, I went home, and, gratefully, found that my key worked. I got back in my house, picked up a book, and read for the rest of the day. I was happy to be getting away. Too many messages. Too many prompts to get at it. I was exhausted. We would leave tomorrow if the gate cooperated.

CHAPTER XXI

Ready to Go

*My breath seemed to be way ahead of me. It crossed the sea long
before my body did.
It traveled stealthily,
Silent and cunning, on feathered paws.
Then my heart got up and left me standing there.
I was abandoned on the beach,
Menaced by weathered icons that rolled in with the tide.*
From the Dream Journal of Fiona Elizabeth Kelly

I dreamed again. This time I was standing under an enormous, dark sky festooned with stars, animated by dramatic, darting meteors that plunged toward the sea. When I looked down at my feet, the beach was a rust color and rutted with mean channels filled with dark, standing water that looked very much like run off from a mine. As far as I could see, all the beach foliage was dead or dying. To my right was a weathered shack, its floor also filled with this brackish, motionless water.

Suddenly the ground beneath my feet began to move. At first it seemed only a gentle stirring, but then the earth turned syrupy. The shack began to sink. Trees down beach were falling. There was a hush and then a hellish wind that knocked me over and into the gritty slime. At the same time, flocks of birds rose screaming from the jungle behind me. The birds were in flight above me as the dark turned to bright daylight. The flash hurt my eyes and the birds began to fall, by dozens, into the ocean.

Then the sky above me turned a sickening, electric green, then yellow, and then orange. As I watched, an enormous red fireball formed. On the horizon, far away, I saw what must have been an explosive volcanic eruption. A plume of thick ash, which I took to contain gases and vapors that would quickly kill all plant and animal life in its immediate vicinity, rose quickly, miles into the air above.

Even as I watched this new horror, the two dogs approached me. They approached me gently. I was still lying in the muck as they each placed a paw on arm and looked at me with a look that could only be called pleading.

CHAPTER XXII

Launch!

We live on a placid island of ignorance in the midst of black seas of infinity, and it was not meant that we should voyage far.
H.P. Lovecraft

I woke up early the next morning, while it was still dark, and I was groggy and troubled by my dream. Yet, there was the excitement of leaving! I couldn't quite believe it. We were really ready. Anui called on his cell phone from inside a "le truck" he had mounted somewhere near his house. He wanted to leave his scooter at his house while we were gone. "Le trucks" were a sort of bus with wooden cabins with rows of benches and windows built on the flatbeds of trucks. Their windows were just framed openings, so they were breezy and fun to ride but had no definite schedule that I'd been able to figure out. Anui was on his way to the canoe, he said. He had done his final personal packing and said the weather looked good. No problem.

Emere rang up shortly after. It was 4:30 a.m. She was going out to the bank of the stream that ran behind her property to catch a few fish for breakfast, and then she would join us at the canoe. After my first visit to her house, I knew how much she liked to eat those little lagoon fish fresh from the water. It was an economical way to fish. She used a length of less than a one pound test line and a smallish hook with a little bit of bait. She tossed the line and hook out, a few feet from where she stood, and within ten minutes or so she pulled in sufficient fish for a breakfast or dinner. The banana leaves she wrapped them in kept them cool and fresh. It was a habit she enjoyed. This would be her last lagoon fish for a few days, and she would not be hurried away from these tasty morsels.

I checked and rechecked my watertight bags and made sure the gate opened and the car started. Then I went back in for my own breakfast: a bowl of melon, bananas, pineapple, and yogurt. It was pretty much what I ate at home, but, needless to say, the fruit was far fresher and better tasting here.

My duffels were really dry bags designed for running rivers and keeping the water out of one's belongings. They folded down several times on top then folded and clipped shut to make a tight closure. I stuffed everything deep into the bags. I had a few tee shirts and shorts, a pair of flip-flops, and an emergency blanket that could double as a signal flag if you waved its bright, metallic side about. I had sun block, mosquito repellent, ibuprofen and aspirin, some small mirrors for signaling, a flashlight that had a loud whistle built into one end, spare batteries, a mosquito net hat, a deck of cards, a travel version of Mexican Train, two neck scarves with evaporating coolant built in, toothbrush and paste, soap, a quick-dry, light-weight travel towel, moisturizer, a couple of Sarah Waters books in their own waterproof bags, a sketch pad, and some pastel pencils. No reason to take chocolate. It would melt. No reason to take electronic devices. They wouldn't work. But Emere was bringing a GPS she'd gotten a couple of years ago. It would give us coordinates and help us track ourselves and our own movements…and get us back to where we had been if we got lost. That was assuming the GPS actually worked and we could keep it stocked with AA batteries.

Once I had tasted breadfruit, I had no doubt that we would have all the food we'd need. Baked lightly, it is like a combination of pudding and custard and *crème* caramel. It wouldn't take much to cook it in our little improvised oven heated by the onboard fire pit. It has lots of carbs and some vitamin C. With that and the other fruits we were bringing and fresh fish every day, we would be fine. I tucked in cinnamon and some newly dried vanilla from a local plantation, a few tablespoons of dried Hatch chilies, and a shaker of Tabasco. You can't be too safe.

Phad was eager to get going when I called at his house and bade him come into the car. His owners, Henri and Loretta, had won a weaner pig at a bingo game and had given the runty thing Phad's doghouse. Phad was living in the backyard of the restaurant now where he could not observe the passing parade of tourists and townspeople. He simply loved growling, snapping, and barking from the end of his strained leash. (He was only occasionally on this leash. He usually kept his own counsel with regards to comings and goings.) Tourists, who did not know him, cringed and moved further down the street quickly. He liked that they found him annoying and scary. So life at the rear of the Le Grand Thon had been pretty dull for Phad for the past week or so. He had grown to hate the pig.

When I stopped by, Henri and Loretta were up already, baking the day's cakes and breads and croissants. Loretta, who had hurt a buttock muscle in her Tahitian dance class the day before, limped out as Phad jumped in the back seat. She carried a long sack with five baguettes and a big bag of croissants, fresh out of the oven. She also had cut us a big hunk of local goat cheese, the best in the world. We did the French cheek-kissing thing as Henri came out of the kitchen, covered with flour, waving and making grand kissing gestures.

"Okay, Phad," I said. "We're off."

Anui and Emere were at the canoe by the time I pulled in. I parked, pulled on the brake, made sure my lights were out, and picked up my dry bag, a gallon jug of water to add to the supply, and the croissants and baguettes. Phad's kibble was already on board.

We were all excited and stumbling in the still predawn light.

Neighbors and friends came drifting in. News had gotten around that this was the day we would leave, and they were there to put shell necklaces around our necks to assure our return, and to sing, to kiss, to softly shake hands. They were also there to help launch the canoe. Magnolia arrived on a scooter, gigantic purple muumuu flapping around her legs and long shell earrings bobbing. She had a large Graflex Speed Graphic camera strapped to her back. It was easily out of the 1940s. She took out pad and pen. She scribbled a few notes then set up her camera and began shooting pictures. The old fashioned flashbulbs popped loudly and switched out preloaded backs, apparently preloaded with 4" by 5" film sheets, every couple of minutes.

I saw Anna Marie's entire group arrive. They were dressed in their white robes and carried tambourines. It was a party atmosphere as the first light began to brighten the sky and stars began to fade.

Suddenly, we heard a screech or scream from low on the mountain side, across the road, and out of the mass of unruly greenery there. Everyone stopped to look. Out of the tangle of the jungle bower came a human figure. It ran across the street, just visible under a lamp post and barely missing being run over by an early morning scooter commuter.

We could see then that this was a person who, on first glance, seemed to be neither wholly female nor wholly male, although she looked a little like Sigourney Weaver. A *mahu*! Maybe. But this person, *mahu* or not, was ragged, and her crest of hair was wild and matted like a Ceylonese holy woman. It was so thick you could imagine finding Amelia Earhart in there somewhere if you picked around long enough. Her arms and legs were covered with tattoos, and around her neck hung beautiful tiny shells that shone like diamonds in the now rising sun. She was tallish and wiry and moved in a jerky fashion. Her ribs showed through her skin, but the skin itself was firm, and the muscles of her arms and abdomen were taught and healthy looking. She had a half pareo tied on one side, fastened with a slotted, carved, shell. The pareo came to just above her knees. On each wrist she wore shell bracelets with several boars' teeth in the mix. In one hand she had a small parcel or canvas sack about the size of a messenger bag. It could not have contained much. In the other hand, she held a mask made of a large polished coconut shell and carefully incised with symmetrical swirls and hooks. The mask just covered her face when she held it before her. When she was unmasked, her eyes were flashing a deep amber. She approached us directly. I could see now she was a she and not a *mahu*. Though she was wild and unkempt, I could see she was a quite beautiful person, definitely biologically female, probably in her late fifties. Maybe older.

"I will go with you," she said, as if we had asked her many times and now she had conceded to our wishes.

"I will go," she repeated. She tossed her canvas bag into the canoe, stood at the bow, facing the sea, and began to incant:

Roll on great waves.
Break on the voyagers with an
Earth-splitting roar.
Bite them with forked lightening.
Toss them over foaming surf.
Show them the anger of devouring wild dogs.
But then recede with the tides and give them your will and strength.

This was all very impressive, but curious. I thought perhaps this woman had some kind of classical education or had read some of the same articles I had about Moa Nui. Something about the chant was familiar. Maybe it was quoted in Henrietta Poussiere's work, I wondered.

This launch was a little looser than the one Anui had experienced just a few years earlier when he took off on his own. Still, I noticed that some people were raking the beach and picking up the few pieces of rubbish scattered about. This would do for the "cleansing." Everyone was eager to help. Some of the elders were calling out warnings or advice to us. Some were just joking and teasing Anui about the trip. People came forward as we stood near the canoe and kissed us on both cheeks while placing shell necklaces over our heads. Someone began drumming, but softly. Even the local ukulele teacher was strumming and singing *My Island Home*. A few elder aunties cried. The local women's dance troupe, including Loretta, appeared from nowhere and began their routine. Some of them giggled. All of them were earnest.

Magnolia asked the dance troupe to pose along side the outrigger with us. Then she made several photos and wrote down each person's name on her pad.

The eldest man and woman began the purification ceremony. Everyone settled down when they stepped forward. I knew a little about what was going on because of Anui's description of what happened before his journey. The canoe was lifted into the water, nose first, by strong arms. It settled there while the elders directed that the sea salt be placed in everyone's hands, then under their tongues, and then on the nose of the canoe. The newcomer stepped forward, lifted her arms into the air, and invoked the spirits of the ancestors. No one challenged her authority to do so, even though she was much younger than the elders present. A local ecology professor, who taught in the high school, gave a short talk about which plants had been used to make the canoe. He told about which ones were endangered and how important it was to treat all the native plants with respect. A first grade class from the local school stood together to sing with the ukulele teacher. It was another version of *My Island Home*. Then each child presented us with flowered headdresses and tossed flowers all around and into the canoe. Emere was given an offering to toss overboard as we left the beach. We were told to paddle to the east first, and then follow the currents. As many men and women who could grab the gunwales lifted the canoe further into the water and we were off.

The sun came up just as *Cum Sancto Spiritu* from Bach's Mass in B Minor began playing on someone's boom box. The piece had been cued up by one of the more fervent female representatives of the local Episcopal Church. It was meant to send us on our way under the protection of a Christian god. Here, at last, was a Christian person who recalled her purpose.

Cum Sancto Spiritu
In gloria dei patris.
Amen.
With the Holy Spirit and the glory of God the Father. Amen.
We thanked everyone and set off.

CHAPTER XXIII

A Warning: By Our New Companion

(Who turns out to be called Gertrude)

Preface:

*If there be angels in the deep
Then surely there are devils:
One sure and sleek,
One calm and meek,
An endless chase and run for cover.*

Refrain:

*Defying currents, needle fish conspire.
Two bullet trains, they charge through deep defiles,
And swallow many others' dreams and hopes.
They unnerve fishlets fairly free of guile.*

*If Jesus wore a Crown of Thorns like these,
Equipped with lots of tricks up many sleeves,
A predatory starfish would have been
The symbol that brought Christians to their knees.*

*And then the mantas, bombers of the deep,
A whisper, just a shadow of a face.
They curve themselves with geometric knowledge
An almost-not-bound Thing in time and space.*

Grim eye-balled beasts that slither out of holes!
Some long white things that look and leave no trace.
Pursuer or pursued? They cannot know.
They stay at home most days in ignorance.

And then the fish that chooses to disguise
And cringes on the bottom with a plan
To kill whatever ventures near and touches
His musty visage bears a Little Grin.

I liked the part about the Crown of Thorns starfish, I told her. It really was something to think about one of those on Jesus' head and what my grandmother's crucifixes, one over every door of her house, would have looked like with such a creature embellishing them.

I continued to wonder about Gertrude's sources.

CHAPTER XXIV

Day One

It still amazes me how many millions goes to discovering another star in the galaxies when, for all we know, we are sitting on top of another undiscovered world beneath our feet.
Martin Dansky

The sun was up now, and the water of the lagoon reflected pink and yellow as we headed toward the reef. It didn't take long for the relatively cool morning breezes to subside and the heat to begin. It was going to be a fairly cloudless morning, and the seas looked calm before us. I pulled off my tee shirt and shorts and stripped down to my bathing suit. Emere wore a brightly patterned pareo tied at her waist and hugging just above the knees and a flowered bikini top. We were already sucking at our water bottles.

A pod of dolphins appeared just to our starboard side. Their brilliant, black bodies shone in the light. Phad made little barking noises as he watched them. They played near us, jumping up to tease Phad occasionally, until we reached the reef itself. It was sheer bliss to watch them play and feel part of it. Then a team of black-tipped reef sharks took over. Phad growled, but then politely and wisely moved a little more to the center of the canoe and flattened himself. There were still little rumbles coming from him, but he did not look over again. The sharks herded us out of the channel. We were leaving the safety of the lagoon now and heading for the open sea. And Phad was learning to be a good citizen and a sailor.

I was exhilarated. My pulse was pounding, and I discovered that I had a broad grin on my face. It was a kind of happiness I had never remembered feeling before. This was a joy that spread from my toes to the roots of my hair. It spread like a Fourth of July sparkler from the tip of my spine to the base of my skull. It was a joy mixed with thrill, excitement, an almost fear of the unknown, an almost envy of my own exalted sense of adventure. We were on the journey. And yet all these feelings were mixed with the certainty that we had very real work to do, and there would be difficult challenges to meet. There was no way to share all these feelings, but I caught Emere's eye and I knew she was with me.

After we breached the reef, I began to breathe normally again. I remembered my yoga and calmed myself, my heart rate, and my racing monkey brain. We looked at each other, Emere, Anui, and I, and laughed out loud all at once.

Then we looked at our new member. We asked her about herself and we found out that her name was Gertrude and that she was a poet. She said it was her job to be with us, to orate, to remember what we did, to turn it into song and chant, and to impersonate the spirits when it might be helpful to do so. Her work, she said, was to overwhelm the enemies or whatever the hell we met with words and with her frightening visage, alarming limbs, frightening adornments, dreadful hairdo, and gap-toothed smile. Her look, she said, she had carefully cultivated from a young age once she understood her talents and gifts. She was an orphan and had been raised by old people who knew the ancient ways. She had dreams beginning at age nine. When the old folks died, she took care of herself. She didn't mind, she said. It was her destiny to be a prophet, and prolonged periods of isolation were useful to her development. Someone in every community had to do this work, and fate chose her.

She promised that in time she would tell stories and even jokes to earn her keep on our journey. She also promised to recite new verses regularly. But, for now, she was busy composing poems in her head and reciting them to herself so that she would be able to tell everyone back home about the trip. This, she said, would make a far better record than handwritten journals, sketchbooks, or photographs. Better, she opined, to use language to describe and to commit that language to memory in the presence of the phenomena one apprehended and wished to recall later.

She told us that she had read Cicero as a child and was particularly impressed by the story of Simodedes of Ceos and the use of the memory palace as an aid for recollecting detailed information. She also worked on her speech using a method she learned from studying Plutarch and the story of Demosthenes putting pebbles in his mouth. She was also a fan of Chief Dan George, she said. She had seen all of his films with her adoptive parents. Her personal favorite was *Little Big Man* followed by *The Outlaw Josey Wales*. She had carefully followed George's spoken indictments of white colonialism and his role in first nation politics in Canada.

The beauty of the trees,
The softness of the air,
The fragrance of the grass,
Speaks to me,
And my heart soars.

This was among her favorites of quotes from Dan George. She recited it several times on the trip.

We had no sooner finished thinking about Chief Dan George and Canada when we spotted a small, yellow zodiac inflatable to our port side. We had only been out an hour or so, but were already in a strong current pulling us toward our destination. Anui had been consulting charts, and he and Emere had been working the sails. All aboard was in good order, and we had already been planning our evening meal: breadfruit cooked right on our on-board fire pit. It would be allowed to blacken on one side, then flipped, then cut open and sliced into a pan of bubbling oil. We would make an avocado dip with fresh tomato salsa and lightly pan fry tuna and sear some eggplant with garlic. Tonight, we would make Grey Goose martinis with just a hint of vermouth and, of course, two or three pimento stuffed olives each. Gertrude said she would be glad to wash the dishes if we did all the cooking. Living alone most of her life, she had not the skill to cook for more than one. And, she said, she lived mostly on raw fruits and the occasional fish. Emere preferred to mix the drinks. Anui didn't care. He would build and tend the fire and cook if I acted as *sous* chef. That meant I had to be ready to do anything.

As we were discussing all these attractive possibilities for the evening, the yellow zodiac moved in closer, and we could see now that there was a sturdy-looking, yellow-haired, fair-skinned woman on board alone. She hallooed us and waved a red bandana in the air. It seemed to be tied to a long stick…or…or…it was a bow! Like a violin bow, only bigger. We pulled closer until we could grab the ropes on the zodiac and haul her in. It *was* a bow, a cello bow, and Lygia, for that was her name, came aboard lugging her cello behind her.

CHAPTER XXV

Lygia Comes Aboard

I have come to believe that the whole world is an enigma, a harmless enigma that is made terrible by our own mad attempt to interpret it as though it had an underlying truth.
Umberto Eco

Lygia was in surprisingly good shape considering that, according to her tale, she had set off on her own from a marina in Hilo, Hawaii some days or weeks ago. (That part was unclear.) She had left port with only a ham sandwich, a mixed box of plum flower, strawberry, and sweet potato mochi from the Uchida sisters' Two Ladies Kitchen (A Hilo classic.), five boxes of Pulmuone Instant Naengmyun noodles (She could, she said, tolerate MSG.), and a plastic container filled with five gallons of fresh water. She had not, of course, intended to be adrift but was lost and blown away from the Big Island when an unexpected squall interrupted her day of sightseeing and frustrated her plan to camp on an isolated beach along the coast. Her thought was to stay at least a couple of nights on a solo retreat and use the time to compose a new cello sonata. She was well known for her music at home and was known locally as "Yo-Yo Mama." Her instrument was a reproduction of the 1733 Montagnana cello from Venice that Yo-Yo Ma himself plays. Her business cards bore the image of a cello crossed with an image of a vintage Duncan yo-yo. She was also a trained conductor, and thus her business cards also offered "super-conductivity" upon request. She was always busy.

On her way to the campsite, she had been distracted making photographs of sea birds and the shoreline and didn't notice the approaching storm that soon brought a heavy downpour. With the rain came a miserable mist and fog that settled low over the sea. Nothing could be seen beyond about five feet of the boat.

Being a sensible woman from the Canadian maritime, indeed from Fogo Island, Newfoundland, she knew how to handle the boat, and she knew quite a bit about how to survive at sea. Her drop pearl earrings had lovely, large hooks that held them to her pierced ears. They could easily be baited and pull in small fish. She wore a couple of large bracelets she had picked up in a street market in northern Thailand. Their various components were held together by fish line. That would do nicely, and, with the hooks, she had perfect gear for jigging. Mochi would have to do for bait at first with maybe a bit of ham. After she had caught one fish, she had more bait to cut. She figured she could simply recycle fish bodies *ad nauseam* if need be.

The old Fogo men had taught her when she was just a child how to distill fresh water from seawater. In addition to her overnight camp gear, she wore a camel pack around her waist. It had two reservoirs for extra water! But more important to her desalination plan was the tubing from the camel packs. She could expose one reservoir to bright sunlight and let the water evaporate through the tube into the other. With luck, she'd be able to capture any rain water in a fold of her emergency windbreaker. That would be an invaluable aid to hydration in the very unlikely case that she would be at sea long enough to use up her current water supply and that she was able to desalinate.

She had a pup tent in her pack. She had wrapped her cello in a large, Ziploc-type bag, but she used the pup tent to protect it further from sun and heat. She figured she could use her Sterno stove to cook if she were careful, and she had extra canisters of fuel.

Little did she imagine how long she would be on her own.

Still, she set out preparing for the worst, for, when the clouds and mist cleared, there was no sign of a shoreline in any direction. She began fabricating, arranging her belongings, and inventorying the supplies that came with the rented zodiac. She realized she should have done this before she left for her camp-out. Now, however, she was pleased with what she found: a sealed pocket at one end of the craft that contained an emergency pouch of drinking water, basic first aid kit, anti-seasick tablets, a whistle with a lanyard, a 2400 calorie ration pack, a hatchet, a zodiac repair kit, a signal mirror, a jack knife, a large tube of SPF 70 sun block, a rescue quoit, and a manual encased in a red plastic pouch entitled "How to Survive at Sea." It was written in Chinese, English, and French. Two of these languages she could read.

Of course, she had two oars, but only a ten horsepower motor and very little gasoline. Still, survival didn't seem a problem. She reckoned that if Thor Heyerdahl or whomever could sail across the Pacific in a raft made of balsa and mangrove, she could do the same with this much sturdier little boat and these ample supplies.

So she slathered on the sun block, drank some water, and got out her cello. The squall had passed, the sea was calm, and the sun was out. In many ways, she was delighted with her predicament. She played during the day under the shelter she had rigged up with the pup tent and ground cloth. She rinsed out her clothes every day and wore them wet so the evaporating water would cool her. She kept her Aussie style outback hat on and her skin well-greased. And she played. Sometimes a dolphin would hear her, or a whole herd, and follow behind the zodiac for miles, leaping and grinning. They clearly loved this unusual sight and the lovely melodies the human produced. Unlike great white sharks, they preferred classical.

She ate her rations, holding some back for the days she didn't have much fishing luck. She told herself stories and recited the collected works of William Shakespeare, learned from years at the knee of her sainted Irish grandmother. She assumed the voices of different characters and pretended to be watching a stage play. She remembered him writing:

Fishes live in the sea, as men do a-land; the great ones eat up the little ones.

She spent a full 24 hours, she guessed, trying to remember the rest of the speech and where it came from. Then, she remembered the dialogue:

"*Master, I marvel how the fishes live in the sea.*"

"Why, as men do a-land. The great ones eat up the little ones: I can compare our rich Misters, to nothing so fitly as to a whale; he plays and tumbles, driving the poor fry before him, and at last devours them all at a mouthful."

Finally, it came to her. *Pericles, Prince of Tyre.* It had fishermen in it, she was sure now. Someone had staged the play at the Newfoundland Shakespeare by the Sea festival once years ago. The director had used only local fishermen for the roles of sailors, pirates, fishermen and messengers and selected ones with particularly heavy brogues in the hope that their pronunciation of English more closely matched the Elizabethan era English. The director also managed to entice Joey Smallwood, the premier of Newfoundland and Labrador at the time, to play the role of Pericles. It is imperative that Pericles wear a suit of armor in the second or third act of the play, she recalled, and the festival had only an outfit suitable for a man in the six foot range. The "little fellow from Gambo" could hardly see and then only from the mouthpiece of the costume by standing on tiptoes. He dragged the costume across the stage in slow motion, though he was intended to portray Pericles in battle. The audience roared with laughter and egged the peppery little fellow on. "Give it to 'em, Joey," they screamed. The point of the play was, of course, lost, though it must be said that the people on The Rock seldom did get the point, if there was one. Nor did they care to get the point. They could always make up their own. This creative response to deprivation was the thing Lygia loved most about her people. They really attended the festival in those days just to break the monotony of life largely devoid of children and grandchildren. Joey, at whom they happily laughed, had sent them "away" as part of his ambitious scheme to resettle the population.

And thus, in memory and thought, Lygia passed the days at sea. She wrote not only one, but six sonatas. She lost a little weight. She made an entire deck of playing cards out of paper in her journal and then played a lot of solitaire, crouched inside the pup tent so that the "cards" would not be blown into the sea.

The day before we found her, she actually had a chance at rescue. The cruise ship Paul Gauguin passed very near her. She could have signaled to be taken aboard, but the thought of leaving her little zodiac and joining an elder hostel, or "road scholar" voyage, as they were now called, actually sickened her. She didn't relish roaming decks full of people with large diamond rings who had paid eleven thousand dollars to recreate the expeditions taken by European adventurers and imperialists. There was something odd about this, she mused. She knew they would be talking about pearl shops and their grandchildren and comparing digital cameras and the size of their lenses. No, no, no. She decided to take her chances and let the Paul Gauguin puff by on its way to Moa Nui. No one really noticed her, anyway. The tourists and crew were gathered in a great lounge, cocktails in hand, enjoying a luncheon lecture on the *marae* archaeology. They were anticipating their landing at the Moa Nui quay. They had a full afternoon planned. It would begin by a trip to see the alarming, pink-eyed, giant groupers that hung out just west of the island. They could easily be lured to perform with the offer of a can of mackerel. Each tourist was equipped with one. The excursion would end with a trip to a black pearl farm where most of the women planned to drop a few thousand.

As the Paul Gauguin lumbered by, "something else will come along," Lygia thought to herself. She drew her bow across her strings in a dramatic *portato* stroke, focusing on the rotation of her left hand, and allowed her craft to drift on. Thus, in the middle of an exercise in *staccato/legato* reversals, she was found and taken aboard.

Although Lygia's journey of over a thousand miles may seem unlikely, it has been done before. Probably people have drifted this distance across the Pacific many times. Heyerdal crossed 7,700 kilometers of the Pacific in the Kon Tiki. That's nearly 5,000 miles.

There is an account in Poe's book, *Gordon Arthur Pym*, of the brig Polly that left Boston on December 12, 1811. She was caught up in a huge storm. The ship was torn to shreds, her masts ripped away. The survivors of this mayhem were found 191 days later, having drifted over 2000 miles. Lost at sea, one is, of course, at the mercy of the elements. Lygia rode the waves, suffered rainstorms, gusts, and agonizing heat. She was sometimes hungry but never really thirsty. She was lonely at times and missed her family. She worried about them, knowing they would assume her dead. Or maybe not. They knew she was resourceful and plucky. They might not give up on her. And there were many good days. Those were the days when she saw flying fish or flocks of seabirds or magnificent night skies and sunsets. No, it was not all bad.

CHAPTER XXVI

Gertrude Chants a Canoe Spell

Gertrude's eloquence continues to surprise me. Her words remind me of something Umberto Eco wrote in The Island of the Day Before. However, I can't remember what it was.
From the Journal of Fiona Elizabeth Kelly.

Let our cordage not ravel,
Let our caulk hold tight
As gaily we travel
All through the night

Braid it right, then braid once more,
Then inside and outside and take it fore.
Tie it then
And around again,
Then twice 'round a hook, fast on the floor.
It will hold you true
In your quick canoe.
And the waves will part
Through the surf you'll dart.
Ah, cordage, good cordage,
Comment ça va?

That first night out, we were all too excited to sleep, even though we were exhausted from the day. Gertrude made us stay alert through the twilight. She warned that the most spiritually dangerous and powerful times of day are those betwixt and between periods of dusk and dawn. She said that substances like honey, neither solid nor liquid, and people like her, neither wholly male nor female in spirit, were equally powerful. So we listened and watched and waited quietly while the light faded. Then we lit a few lamps and settled in for the evening.

Although I'd been on Moa Nui for several days, I hadn't really been outside past around midnight. The skies I saw overhead on this first night at sea, from far beyond land, ocean, were astonishing. Even with a bright moon, just a few days from full, the stars were brilliant masses above us. I was more accustomed to picking out Northern Hemisphere constellations, so the thousands of objects visible in these dark, unpolluted skies threw me.

What I first picked out of what seemed chaos was the marvelous Milky Way. It crossed the sky, north to south. As I looked south, I could make out the bright stars called "The Pointers." These are *Hadar* and *Rigil Kentauri*. I followed them and saw the Southern Cross. It was not obvious to me at first because it was lying on its side. Once I made out the Southern Cross, I shouted to the others and we all began calling out new finds. We found *Centaurus* and *Hydra* that night. Someone found the *Triangulum Australe* and Anui pointed out the Toucan. It was left to Gertrude to point to the Chameleon. It was late before we drew lots for first watch and stopped chattering. Phad had long since begun to snore.

CHAPTER XXVII

Day Two

In Which We Meet the Sperm Whale

All that most maddens and torments; all that stirs up the lees of things; all truth with malice in it; all that cracks the sinews and cakes the brain; all the subtle demonisms of life and thought; all evil, to crazy Ahab, were visibly personified, and made practically assailable in Moby Dick. He piled upon the whale's white hump the sum of all the general rage and hate felt by his whole race from Adam down; and then, as if his chest had been a mortar, he burst his hot heart's shell upon it.
Moby Dick, Herman Melville

There is nothing in the sea or indeed on the land so grand as a sperm whale. Most of those who have dabbled in English and American literature have met the great albino sperm, Moby Dick, the nemesis of Captain Ahab. What, I wonder, does a reader learn about the whale from Melville's 1851 depiction? The image of the bitten-leg of Ahab is surely one that even the casual reader retains. It may not be considered that Moby Dick had very good reason to bite the man's leg off. If the story is read as a mere tale of man against nature, then surely men will always root for men. Environmentalists, wildlife biologists, and Greenpeace activists usually take the other side. A few of the liberal stripe may root for the animals over their coffee and biscuits but do very little on their behalf beyond a trip to an aquarium now and then.

Old Moby was based upon the story of a real whale. Well, as real as one could credit in the 1800s. There were no photographs of the creature until later. The first picture of it underwater was taken in 1953 and appeared in Life magazine. Hans Hass was traveling with whalers in the Azores. He paddled about in a small boat until, after day of vigilance, a whale headed right for him. He dropped overboard and dove down forty-five feet. He captured an image of a sixty-five foot long male, "pock-marked by years of battle with his favorite food...the giant squid." The fabulous animal passed within twenty feet of Hass. The photograph shows an unsmiling, enormous, grey presence. It is truly a masterful beast. But in the 1800s, there were no such images and no real knowledge of the whale in its habitat. The earliest I know of is an albumin print from about 1890. Four sturdy men stand solemnly on a ship's deck around the head of a very dead and relatively small sperm whale. Nobody in the picture appears to be happy. Least of all, the whale.

So the sperm whale and ideas about its might and size was just a story that leapt from boat to boat and mouth to mouth. Like the distortions that occur in the telephone game, the ferocity and capabilities of the whale were exaggerated in the telling. The Moby Dick story was the one oft told: a crazed, white, bull sperm that liked to attack ships for sport. Who knows why the stories were believed, because their sources were not the most reliable. For example, these same tale-tellers thought there were great monsters in the sea and that most of the world's indigenous people were busy eating each other at a rate that would have killed them all off in a generation or two. Either that or they were said to be trotting about stark naked without work or religion. So who is to say how the story of the white bull sperm stuck? Still, with the publication of Melville's book, the story of the behemoth and the utter destruction it wreaks is one that informs the hearts and minds of many modern people if he or she considers the sperm whale at all.

The sperm is a lively, enormous (reaching a length of nearly 70 feet and can grow to weigh as much as 60 tons) creature that typically dives over three thousand feet in quest of a juicy giant squid. It can go deeper—much deeper. I cannot think why one would pursue such a strange looking thing as a squid for food, except that the giant squid is very, very big, and the sperm whale has an enormous appetite. The giant squid can grow to over forty feet long. It stays in the deep. It has a mantle, eight arms and two much longer tentacles. It can do lots of damage with these limbs.

The arms are lined with suction cups and the cups are ringed with sharp teeth like protrusions. It is hard to imagine being wrapped in such arms without suffering massive injury. However, a squid does have a lot of squid fun down in those dark waters in spite of their toothy appendages. They apparently enjoy amorous contact with those of their own sex. The squid is, of course, not alone in its proclivity. Giant squids also have the largest eyes of any creature on the earth and other sensory devices that enable it to operate, for a mollusk, with cunning and precision.

The sperm whale cares nothing about these facts. It is interested only in the caloric content of said squid. The sperm whale dives, presumably adjusting its buoyancy with the spermaceti encased within its large head along with its enormous brain, and stays submerged, if it wishes, for over, an hour. That gives it plenty of time to sneak up on a squid and eat it. As it travels below the surface, it whistles, clanks, burbles and bubbles, its echoing vocalization perhaps letting other sperm whales miles away know what it is up to and where it is, and these noises, and resultant echoes, are useful in locating food sources.

It travels in pods—at least females and babies do—and that was what we met up with: a very nice, lively pod of sperm whales. There were nine members, and they stayed around us, rolling, tumbling, shallow diving, blowing, breaching, and generally frolicking for a good forty-five minutes. Gertrude chanted and Lygia played. We felt incredibly lucky. The eyes. I could swear those eyes were telling me stories. They were small but incredibly intelligent. The calves, though already checked and crusty in places, sported beautiful belly folds and soft, almost white-looking skin one could imagine caressing. They were careful not to menace or present us with any cause for worry. They maneuvered around us carefully keeping fins and great dark fans of flukes in check.

I knew we were on the right journey after this lovely morning.

CHAPTER XXVIII

Day Three: The Odyssey by Gertrude

Set to Music by Lygia

Arranged for Three Voices, Cello, and Oboe

The first to come were floating mouths
With grinning lips and startling eyes.
They came adrift from out the south
And woke us with their skittery cries.

The chief one had an entourage
With slightly smart-assed things to say.
They cut us dead and begged, "fromage!"
We tossed them cheese; they went away.

The next up were the drumming moths.
They boomed and thumped to samba rhythms.
They did this all while still aloft,
Refracting light much like a prism

The biggest wanted all our bread.
We tossed our baguettes on the sea.
The smallest wanted all our heads.
"Just bugger off," we yelled with glee.

The next to come were smiling pickerels.
They circled round a couple times
Then asked for rhymes with nothing literal.
We thought, of course, of Gertrude Stein.

A shell encrusted albatross
(A nasty bit of feathered beast)
Came telling us that all was lost.
We rang his neck and had a feast.

Some vengeful Pomeranians,
Deranged and very spiteful,
And very nice Ukrainians
Came a-begging mouthfuls
Of hands or thighs or even butts.
We knew they didn't have much guts,
So quickly we dispatched the mutts.

One rainy day we saw a plover.
Alas, it had a claw like fang.
It bit and snatched; we ran for cover,
Then, to our surprise, it sang.

A mildewed dolphin came to call,
Great clumps of seaweed made its hair.
We thought that we had seen it all,
But suddenly it wasn't there.

This fish knew how to disappear
And how to click its teeth in time.
It really never showed much fear
Until it saw us lofting limes.

A frozen walrus, tusk replete
With resplendent inlaid jewels,
Swam through the brine on flippered feet
And led us to some gentle pools.

Lo, there we met with tiny mites
Arrayed in pirate costumes
They bothered us. How they could bite!
They smelled of empty tombs.

They asked us riddles four and ten.
We fell into a stupor,
Then answered all, set sail again
Surrounded by six groupers.

CHAPTER XXIX

Day Four

How to Navigate a Canoe in the Pacific

Twenty years from now you will be more disappointed by the things that you didn't do than by the ones you did do. So throw off the bowlines. Sail away from the safe harbor. Catch the trade winds in your sails. Explore. Dream. Discover.
Mark Twain

We were making great headway and figured we would reach our destination by that evening. We had eaten well, listened to wonderful music and poetry, shared every joke we could remember, and taken time to swim and snorkel as we made our way toward Mauntaerae Island. We still had some distance to go but had started watching for signs of its landmass.

We were using all ancient sailing and navigation techniques. We knew that Leo was directly north-northeast, and *Castor* and *Pollux* were almost directly north. We had observed them at about eleven o'clock the night before we left. That meant we could take their positions the same time each night, have a fair idea of our direction, and make any corrections. We knew that these constellations and stars would take their position about four minutes later each night, and that was helpful. We used a star hook to keep us on the same relative latitude and to keep our course true. We used the brightest star on the horizon before us, *Pollux*, then alternative stars as that first one rose too high. Sirius was by far the brightest star we could see. It was just northwest of us overhead when we took our reckonings.

We also took into account winds, currents, and swells, the location of clouds, and the pattern of sea bird flights, especially toward dusk. But most helpful to setting our course and keeping it were Gertrude's stories and songs. She knew all the features of the landscape of other tiny islands along the way and could point out each crag and outcropping. Even when mists came in and darkness descended, it was she who had memorized ancient navigational current and island charts. She used shells and bits of cord and broken sticks to construct a map of the ocean we would pass over and thus helped Anui remember what he knew about shallow and deep water and particularly important *motus* or small islands we needed to recognize and avoid. She also had memorized the ancient star charts.

Of course, we had Emere's GPS. And we had compasses with us. They would help, but the variation between magnetic and true north would have required careful observation and correction. We had little if any iron in the canoe to confuse a compass. Still, a modern GPS would be more useful if we needed back up. If Gertrude had not come along, we would probably had to have used it. Even so, secretly, so as not to irritate Gertrude, Emere checked the GPS against Gertrude's regular pronouncements. She was always right, and, though it was good to know we had a back-up, it was lovely not to have to really use it. It might help when we got up into the mountain and jungles.

CHAPTER XXX

Landing on Mauntaerae

My life seems to be meant for days like this, the days that seem to help make sense of all the rest. These are the days I'll remember when I'm very old.
From the journal of Fiona Elizabeth Kelly

There it was, just ahead of us on the horizon. We spotted it the afternoon of the fourth day. First, we saw a fluffy cloud in the distance. The interaction of trade winds and local geologic features on islands create convergence zones and complex sea and wind patterns that produce distinctive cloud patterns and rainfall. We knew we were near when we saw that cloud. As we traveled further, we began to see birds in the air. They were too high to identify. Then the noises began: great cries and howls and screeches of wild creatures that, we deduced, lived on the island.

Mauntaerae was formed around a central, ancient volcanic peak. It appeared to be long and irregular in shape with a deep dip in its center. It had a northeast-to-southeast orientation. We quickly estimated its highest point to be around five thousand feet. The peak was flattened on top, somewhat in the shape of Mount St. Helens in Washington State. From this distance at sea, it was dark and dramatic. The entrance to the lagoon was easy to find. We could see the birds more clearly now, but, oddly, there were none that we recognized nor, after gazing at lengthy into the turquoise waters, did we see fish that we'd come to associate with Pacific lagoons.

Surprisingly, there was a wisp of smoke on a beach ahead. We made out that the smoke seemed to be emanating from someone's campfire. Though we still had a half hour or so of light left by the time we were within the lagoon, it was nice to have the fire to aim for. But who could be on this remote and forsaken beach on an island we had been told was long uninhabitable and devoid of human and animal life?

Before we could investigate the fire, we had to land. As we hit the shore, we could see that we were in for an out-of-the-ordinary sojourn. When we hefted the canoe up the beach and began to secure it, each and every gastropod shell on the beach got up and skittered, in a neatly choreographed diagonal direction, toward the jungle margin. This startling parade included quite large conches. It was as if the beach itself was moving, for gigantic and vigorous hermit crabs had wholly overtaken it, the *Paguroidea* that occupied the shells. There were thousands of them. They ran in great alarm while clasping their shells tightly with their abdomens. Uninterrupted competition for shells and the effects, we presumed, of radiation, had selected generation after generation for the largest of these creatures. One was easily as large as a Labrador Retriever, its claws as dangerous looking as a large pair of garden shears. When they reached the jungle edge, they turned, stood upright on their back legs, and began drumming their shells with their pincers.

"Don't mind them," a voice called as we moved warily toward the fire. We saw a middle aged man standing and facing us from out in the water, in front of the flaming pit. He returned to a kneeling position in the tide and seemed to be cleaning something. As we approached him, casting a guarded look now and then toward the crabs, he smiled. He was cleaning a chicken, perhaps for his dinner that night. He said he came from an island four days away and had received a call to come here in a dream. As we compared stories, we realized his island had experienced similarly bizarre events and it had fallen on him, through his dreams, to see what he could do about it.

We returned to secure the canoe, unpack some of our gear, and build our own fire. I stretched and walked a bit to get my land legs. Lygia and Emere decided to do some Yoga. Lygia hadn't been on land for weeks and was wobbly and extremely stiff. We planned a dinner together with Aban, for that was his name. We decided on something that would incorporate the chicken. He was quick to tell us that he had brought several hens from home and showed us the cages and feed he had onboard his own canoe. He said he had already seen wild chickens running about the island but would not advise eating them. Some had snow white feathers. Some had two heads. Some had three feet and many had twice the number of toes on each foot that they should have. He had found an abandoned stone fish trap, but the fish swimming in it had bulging eyes and too many fins. We wouldn't eat them either.

Between the two great canoes, we had all the food we needed for an extravagant dinner. Anui, Emere and Aban directed Gertrude, Lygia and me. Gertrude begged out of kitchen duty in favor of jogging in place and continuing to compose poetry that described what we were doing. Anui and Emere began to dig a large pit in the sand. Aban grabbed some coconuts and pulled out his portable grater. It was cut out of one piece of wood, cleverly hinged so that it folded out into a low seat. On one end it had a half-moon serrated blade. Aban sat down, cracked the coconuts open with his parang, and began grating. He had made a little basket out of palm fronds to receive the gratings. I was sent to gather banana leaves and ferns. We decided they would be safe enough for wrapping or lining the fire pit. I also was sent to gather lava rocks. When Emere and Anui had finished the big pit in the sand, they began collecting firewood.

The chicken would be wrapped in banana leaves, the breadfruit would be put directly on the fire, and several large squashes would be also wrapped cooked in the pit. Among our supplies, Anui found a box of flour with leavening already in it. He added coconut milk squeezed through a piece of loosely woven cloth from the gratings. He threw in some sugar and mixed it all together with his hands. That dough was also wrapped in a large banana leaf. The leaves themselves had been heated then placed in the salt water to make them pliable and to avoid tearing them as we folded them into packets. The center spine of each was flattened by trimming them with a sharp parang. The fire was started and rocks placed on top till they were heated through. Then the food packets were placed on top and covered with ferns then more banana leaves. In a couple of hours, we uncovered the pit and removed our perfectly cooked food. The breadfruit was placed whole on the remaining coals and allowed to blacken on each side before it was split open and the inside fruit sliced.

We made martinis and banana and rum drinks and told each other life stories. The fire kept gnats and mosquitoes away until it was time to sleep under protective nets in our big canoes. The moon was nearly full. It would be full the next night as well, and it was to be a "super moon." The distance between earth and moon varies, and tomorrow night the moon would make its closest pass, within 356, 410 kilometers as opposed to its distance at the far end of its orbit, 407,740 kilometers. Those 51,000 kilometers make a big difference in the moon's apparent size from where we view it on earth. If it is a cloudless, clear night and you are away from city lights, that "super moon" can seem huge and is so bright it makes your eyes pop. There are years between those "super moons" so we took it as a good omen that we would have one in the sky the next evening.

CHAPTER XXXI

A Busy Morning

It was but a light breakfast, however after being skinned, the bird was divided into ten portions, and every man cooked his own as he thought fit, but each did not receive above three mouthfuls.
The Cannibal Islands: Captain Cook's
Adventure in the South Seas, R. M. Ballantyne

Phad woke up first. He barked at a mutant frog-like thing with six-inch-long fingers stemming from his three-inch, rhubarb-red arms and grotesquely swollen body. It had a row of jagged, beet-red protuberances on his back. The fingers were webbed and were an unsightly, mottled green. Phad followed it the length of our beach. At first it jumped like any old frog, but then massive wings that looked like a Japanese fan or *angiospermatic* travelers' palm unfolded from under it, and it flew into a fern-floored forest of *arecaceae* or *palmae*, all draped with a hanging moss. It made a loud buzzing sound as it bounded through the air. As it jumped, its lumpy body and head hung loosely, like a large wattle with eyes, from under the wing structure. When it landed, it looked toward the dog, bared sharp, black teeth, and screamed like an angry possum. Phad was dazzled. He watched for a while, did a play bow, then turned on his heels and darted back to camp barking.

While I watched him coming, I noticed that the moss hanging from the trees was not really moss at all but some kind of furry snake like creature. When the frog arrived and lighted in a clump of fronds, all the moss snakes curled up into tight little balls and moved close into the trunks of the palms. They made a screaming noise that startled both Phad and I. Phad dropped his tail, laid his ears back, and dropped near my feet.

Emere got up at the sound and immediately built a fire from the sticks we'd gathered the night before. Then she pulled her ukulele out of one of her rucksacks in the canoe and started singing *My Island Home*. I was a little rattled by her slightly croaky voice and ragged rhythm so early in the morning, but I noted that I probably needed some coffee before I allowed myself to displace my feelings about this beach and what I'd seen. Furthermore, *My Island Home* is a nice song, I told myself. It is beloved all over the Pacific since Christine Anu's version it hit the charts in the 1990s. Everybody knows it.

Emere hadn't seemed to have noticed Phad and the frog, but she had heard the screams. Now she was playing and singing as if we were on a holiday. Her way of displacing feelings, I figured. Still, it seemed a little odd to me to sing this song here on such a desolate atoll. Maybe she felt she could help dispel the gloom of it all, overcome whatever fear or concern the screams and odd animals had engendered, and reclaim the island for people and life. *My Island Home*, she sang on. Something about it waiting. Something about missing it.

Though this song was written by an Australian for an Australian band, it told the story of so many Pacific islanders displaced by the necessity of economic migration and the complications and demands of colonialism that it became an enormous hit several years ago. Emere must have been thinking about the nuclear tests and how her own family was torn apart when the French took land for nuclear installations. We were seeing the results. We were dealing with the results. And she wanted to be home.

As Emere played and sang, Gertrude and Lygia crawled out of the canoe and immediately began doing Yoga stretches. There was something a little annoying about their dedication to health. I took note again: "I'm grumpy this morning. Gritty all over. Itching all over."

The crabs were still at the edge of the jungle, watching. Anui had been up earlier and came from the direction of Aban's canoe carrying a load of firewood.

After a few morning salutations, Gertrude and Lygia began preparing breakfast for all of us, Gertrude having taken a break from composing. Gertrude had baked more coconut bread overnight in the earth oven. She rustled around in our supplies for a large skillet, hoisted it out of the canoe, set it on a grill over the fire, and began cracking eggs into it. Coffee was set to boil cowboy-style. Just get the water gurgling, remove it from the fire, and tap the right amount of coffee grounds on top. Knock on the side of the pot with a spoon or whatever, and the grounds sink. It is as good a brew as you'll get in any coffeehouse for five bucks a cup. Lygia found fresh banana leaves to use for plates and set a tub of water on a separate fire to boil for cleanup. We still had plenty of food in our coolers. Gertrude got into one of the bigger containers and routed out some guava jam and a big hunk of New Zealand butter for the still-warm bread she had made.

We each had a banana leaf platter covered with a hefty helping of scrambled eggs, and big slices of bread, butter and jam. Gertrude had warmed some slabs of ham after the eggs were cooked. She snipped off big portions for each of us. The coffee was delicious. We flavored it with coconut cream in which we had soaked a vanilla bean. It couldn't have been better. Phad had an extra helping of kibble and a big dish of the fresh water we'd brought with us. Nobody can think on an empty stomach, especially with the threat of crawling chaos all around and double headed roosters competing with themselves to call out the sunrise salute. This was only amusing when they seemed to be attempting to harmonize.

After breakfast, Aban sauntered down beach. He'd been flying a little paper kite and drinking coffee with sweetened condensed milk for the past hour or so. He was very relaxed. When he arrived at our camp, we met over another cup of coffee and discussed our plan for the day. We knew we had to go up toward the top of the island's ancient volcano. That was clear from my dream and all the other signs. Plus, that would be the most spiritually powerful place, one where the ancient population would have gone for messages and guidance.

We decided that Lygia, whose skin was bright red and was already drenched with sweat though it was still early, was not yet acclimatized to land. The decision was that she would stay at the base camp with Gertrude. Gertrude would chant, compose, and say whatever prayers she thought would help. Gertrude and Lygia would keep an eye on everything we would leave below. They would also be charged with keeping an eye on us with signal mirrors. If they kept the fire going, we who were climbing could always follow the smoke if we could see the sky. That would mean sometimes climbing trees to get our bearings. We would have to climb even to see the sun, because the canopy was so thick.

They couldn't let the fire go out. Gertrude and Lygia were backup and our anchors. If we signaled trouble or failed to signal at all, they'd jump in Aban's canoe, and go like hell back to Moa Nui leaving tents, food, water and our canoe for us. We knew Gertrude could handle the navigation and we knew Lygia had the guts and stamina. We didn't plan for that to happen. We had emergency food and overnight gear with us. We packed enough supplies to stay one or two nights in the jungle on our way up if need be. We could use jungle materials for almost everything we needed. We hoped. We had no idea what we might be facing, so we really couldn't plan much beyond that.

I traded my pareo and bare feet for boots, my favorite wicking Smart Wool socks, a pair of cargo pants that could be worn short or long, and a rash shirt. Emere had a similar outfit, but strapped on a parang and threw her musket over her shoulder. She kept her bush hat on but braided her hair and tucked it up into the hat. Anui was bare chested but wore long khakis and a pair of sneakers. He had a sheathed parang hanging from his waist and a Colt Anaconda 44 Magnum double-action revolver tucked into the back of his pant waist with an ammunition belt slung over his shoulder. If we needed help or were in trouble, we would signal with a series of five flares. We'd also fire a series of three to let the folks on the beach know when we were successful. Any other number meant we were using the flares defensively. Emere and I each had several in our backpacks. Aban had a parang for cutting the path but was otherwise unarmed, and he wouldn't trade his shorts for long pants. He had a pair of green canvas army boots on his feet but no socks. He had a camouflage army issue tank top. I had a lightweight sleeping bag and a blow up airline pillow with me. The others brought pareos to use as ground clothes. We had one large mosquito net, one of two we had used on the canoe that we could all fit under. We left the other for Gertrude and Lygia. Aban had some kind of locally made insect repellent, and a batik sarong for his ground cloth.

Before we left, Gertrude asked us to sit in a circle so she could throw the cowrie shells. She did a kind of ceremonial divination using shells she had collected. After her coffee, she had collected four shells. Each had a slit side but the rounded part had been broken off or ground away by coral and wave action. She asked that we each pose a question about our journey and what we might encounter along the way. We didn't have to speak these questions out loud. She would "divine" each of our concerns.

She began with Aban. She tossed the shells after blowing on them. All four shells landed with the open or broken side up. She looked at him directly and said, "You will be safe. You are blessed and protected above all the others. You will bring light to this dark and difficult task."

She turned to me, gathered the shells and tossed again. One shell landed slit side up but the others were open. "Your world is balanced. You sit between heaven and hell, between the living and the dead. Remain open to all the messages for you are the conduit."

Next was Anui. Two of his shells landed slit up and the other two open. She stared at him for what seemed several minutes then tossed the shells again. "Don't ask what you already know," she said to him. He blinked then laughed heartily.

Emere's reading was troubling, at least for me. She had three slits and only one open shell. Gertrude seemed a little quieter and gentler with Emere. "Focus," she said, "on the beam of light in the dark. Do not despair." I knew Emere was just plain homesick. She'd have to get with the program and stop daydreaming.

Lygia, who was to stay on the beach, was confirmed in this. All of her shells landed slit side up. Apparently she had wondered if she really should go up the mountain with us. Gertrude grinned at her and said, "No!" That was very clear.

We rechecked our packs, made sure we had plenty of fresh water, whistled Phad in from his perch on our canoe, and set off.

CHAPTER XXXII

The Long Climb to the Top

...the free fragments in a hollow space included a surprising proportion from organisms hitherto considered as peculiar to far older periods—even rudimentary fishes, mollusks, and corals as remote as the Silurian or Ordovician.
H.P. Lovecraft, At the Mountains of Madness

Almost from the moment we left the beach and entered the forest, the terrain became difficult and the vegetation so thick and heavy I could not imagine how we would pass through it. What wasn't growing from the ground was hanging from the trees, and the tree canopy was so thick that very little light passed through. Even the trunks of the trees supported dozens of life forms: ferns and mosses and wild, almost beautiful blooms that might have been in the orchid family. Then there was the horrid, damp smell. It was the smell of a newly opened grave, and the flowers themselves had a smell reminiscent of a funeral home. The humidity was at nearly 100 percent and the temperature must have been in the high 90s. I was feeling claustrophobic and a bit woozy, but I wouldn't let that stop me.

Aban and Anui went before, slashing and hacking at bizarre shapes and rotting organic matter that defied description. Each hack brought a new pungent odor. Sack-shaped vessels filled with a frothy, yellow, pus-like substance fell and scattered their revolting contents all around us. It splashed onto our shoes and up our legs. When it made contact, it turned from a near liquid to something nearer the consistency of molasses. It was impossible to remove it from our shoes and clothing.

From under leaf-shaped pods, cilia as large as cattails vibrated and sent out clouds of what we took to be pollen. The clouds were thick and orange and lay heavy over our heads. We all hacked and spit, hoping to God we were not being poisoned by the stuff. We quickly pulled kerchiefs up around our faces to cover our noses and mouths. We wished we had brought masks with us. Sunglasses we wore looped around our necks for we had no need of them once we were off the beach, but we all pulled them back on hoping they'd give our eyes some protection from the dust.

Occasionally we caught sight of sinister dark shapes crawling or running low to the ground before us or from each side of our path. Some had feathered or padded feet. Others were apods. All were quick and secretive. From the tall *palmae* and feathered firs hung ropes of the snake moss. There were also long, green tubular plants, at least four inches in diameter, tipped with bright red vents. The vents opened to mouth like cavities that suggested that the tube plants captured whole small animals—that they were indeed some hideous incarnation of a pitcher plant. We examined them closely but carefully and realized that the tubes could swing rapidly in the direction of prey and had both sticky mucus at the opening and a vacuum feature that would suck a victim creature deep into the tube whence it would travel helplessly to some kind of bladder or stomach. There it would be ground to bits, softened with acid, and, ultimately, digested.

We saw rainbow colored snails along our path. They were as big as raccoons and had antennae that rose a foot or two into the air. These twitched and trembled when we passed. Phad was kept close and tended to cower near my feet at the sight and awful smell of it all, for they gave off a fetor that was unworldly. He soon learned not to snap at these monstrous beasts. They were dangerous indeed, for their antennae were really eyestalks topped with swiveling eyeballs. Each stalk bore a series of retractable tentacles that could shoot out at least four feet and in all directions. Phad's nose caught one straight on and he bore a little wound as a reward for his curiosity.

Once we saw a starfish shaped entity that had developed a quartet of pseudo-feet and great pairs of gills between each of its appendages. It was, gratefully, not much bigger than the snails, and we avoided it handily, for we feared it might be as poisonous as a Crown of Thorns, so closely did it resemble that horrid sea being.

Every hour or so, Aban climbed through the tubes and moss snakes, up beyond the tree canopy, and looked in all directions. He could see the smoke and he could flash a mirrored signal below so that Gertrude and Lygia could track our progress. At last he reported the sun was at about 4 o'clock p.m. and that we should clear a spot for a night on the mountain. He judged we had two or three more hours climb to reach the top and we did not wish to arrive in the dark.

Aban and Anui, with the assistance of Emere, cleared a large circle. They used fallen branches and limbs to build a kind of corral inside of which we would rig up our mosquito net, lay our ground cloths, my sleeping bag, and all our gear. We would take turns in pairs staying awake and watching the perimeter of our corral for any intruders.

I was uncomfortable. I didn't have my Thermarest mattress with me, and the ground was lumpy. I got up several times and tossed rocks from out under me. The soil under my bag was uncomfortably damp and gave me a chill. More than once I picked an excessively large ant out of my hair. Though I had a strange chill, the air temperature was as nearly as unbearable at night as was during the day and, everything smelled foul, a combination of earth and rotting vegetation.

The night brought its own surprises. Incredible as it may seem, when the jungle was inky dark, we saw hundreds of iridescent eyes of all sizes and shapes, all trained upon us. I cannot say that these were frightening eyes but more that they were frightened themselves, and even pleading. Between the eyes and the ants, I ended up zipping my bag over my head, mummy style. Then, of course, I nearly smothered from lack of air and the heat.

It was a strange and disturbing journey up this mountain so far, and the horror of it all was really that it was human beings, not any god, that had brought this all into being. With that thought mumbled to one another from our various posts, two of us drifted off to sleep while the others would struggle to remain alert. Well, not Aban. He sat, cross-legged, staring into the jungle, seemingly with no need for slumber.

That great "super moon" was out there, we knew, though we could not see it. Still, it was good to know it was above us. Eerie blades of light and even scattered points made their way through the honeycombed canopy and moved on the forest floor as the moon rose and moved across the sky.

CHAPTER XXXIII

The Next Morning

...tubes tapering from three inches diameter at base to one at tip. Orifices at tips. All these parts infinitely tough and leathery, but extremely flexible.
H.P. Lovecraft, At the Mountains of Madness

I peeked out of my bag early, just as a little light shone through the most eastward trees. I nudged Emere awake. We were immediately dazzled by new wonders and peculiarities. Hanging from trees, seeming to be curious about us, were dozens of *radiata*, symmetrical masses of jelly with *ciliae* projecting and quivering from their central "bodies." These things, we thought, belong in the water, not hanging from trees. They are predators wherever they are found and thus Emere and I, once we registered what we were seeing, jumped to our feet and picked up weapons. The last to draw guard duty in the night, Anui, had fallen asleep on the job. Aban was still in his seated position, but quietly chanting and not at all alarmed. Maybe he could not see these nearly transparent creatures even if he had not been in an, seemingly, altered state.

We approached Anui, still snoring and limbs all akimbo, his pareo in a tangle about his body. We rousted him. He was a bit embarrassed and then saw what had alarmed us.

"Understand," he grunted. He took a warrior's stance.

These bizarre, hermaphroditic *radiata* were a puzzle. How did they come to be here, so far out of the sea? And they were huge, which was also peculiar. But it was only one more to add to the list of enigmas. All around us, since we'd entered the jungle, there were creatures that should be extinct crawling on the ground, creeping through the palms, and flying through the air. It was as if some gigantic molecular clock had been turned on its head.

These *radiata,* for example, are from the *Eumetazoa* kingdom, possibly pre *Ediacaran* Period. That means they could be over 630 million years old! It is a time from which little remains in the fossil record, because most of the creatures were soft and shelless: segmented worms, bare bags and sacs of animals, squishing and mushing themselves through sludge, though some legged things seem to have left tracks. We seemed to be seeing their offspring now, given new life in large form. Maybe a seed, deep within the layers of volcanic matter, was awakened and brought to life. Or perhaps a whole new evolutionary path had been spawned by what awful things had happened on this island.

As restless as we were and as sinister as this all seemed, my scientific mind could not ignore the wonder of what we were witnessing. This was primal life: walking and slithering masses of nerve cells, structureless yet purposeful. Still, I dared not collect or sample. I dared not even touch because, as in the butterfly effect, I might violate a whole unknown system, and I might make matters worse. We packed, I rolled my sleeping bag, and we took down the net. We talked very little, perhaps out of shock, perhaps because each of us needed to work inside ourselves to try to make sense of all we were seeing.

Aban stood, still silent, and made ready to move on. He looked around him and signaled to the rest of us that our corral had been riven on one side. Something had smashed through without any of us knowing, hearing, or seeing. Around and over the places where the enclosure wood had been split asunder was a pungent, prismatic slime. And in that slime, the wood had already begun new growth.

We exited our "safety zone" and as we did, the *radiata* withdrew and other creatures slithered back into the jungle beyond our purview. Anui heedfully propelled himself, limb-by-limb, vine-by-vine, to the top of the canopy to take bearings and send a signal to the beach that we were safe. When he returned, we talked about setting out for the final leg of our trek to the top. We talked for a moment about whether to pull out our Primus stove and make some coffee. We could have. The Primus was one of original design; it was very like if not identical to the one carried by Amundsen, Byrd, and Mallory. That stove was my doing. When I set out for any trek, I always went through a check list of what the very best of adventurers had used successfully. I do not trust the newest or the most innovative in terms of gear, and I certainly don't buy from modern travel retailers who sell throwaway urine cones, air purifiers, and antibacterial wipes. Real travel is not for sissies.

We didn't retrieve the stove from the supply pack. Nobody felt like cooking or even making coffee, so we handed energy bars all around and drank heartily of our safe water supply. I tightened the laces on my vibram-soled climbing boots, rolled my pant legs down around my ankles and clipped them tight, buttoned my shirt sleeves around my wrists, snugged on my bucket hat (a gift from an old WAVE pal), and was ready to follow.

Anui and Aban began cutting a path through the dense jungle as dark and amorphous entities shuddered and withdrew on all sides of us. These formless things seemed somehow to be mocking us. Still, we labored on, sweating in the steamy heat of the claustrophobic vegetation. We were all dripping perspiration. I noticed Aban took out a red bandana and tied it around his brow. At the time I thought this was simply to stop the salty sweat from entering his eyes and blurring his vision. I should have known he was a man whose vision could never be less than crystal clear.

CHAPTER XXXIV

The Trembling Earth

During the climb, I thought more than once about how much more comfortable I'd have been if I'd taken one more trip to REI. How I wished I'd purchased a pair of waterproof socks and a pair of boots with GoreTex. My cheapness undermines my purpose so often.
From the journals of Fiona Elizabeth Kelly

Time stands still, and the earth moves.
For Whom the Bell Tolls, Ernest Hemingway

We picked our path carefully, but it was getting more difficult. The best way forward was almost vertical in places. After about an hour or two of the steep, rocky ascent, we pulled out ropes and clipped ourselves together. We ran a long nylon sling and hooked on to it with our carabineers. It wouldn't do to lose anyone now. The rocks were slippery with unknown substance and damp from the high humidity and a light rain that had fallen in the previous few hours.

We talked very little. Occasionally we had to jump a rill of fast running water. There were rifts and then little terraces now and then. We could pause on these flat areas for a breath. Then we would encounter a steep ravine and sloppy gully where rain had accumulated and the ground had turned muddy, and we would have to scramble up loose talus slopes to get beyond. We mounted escarpment after escarpment—*pali* was what Aban and Anui called these long, steep slopes. Each had its own challenges. It was hard to pick a decent path up to their ridges, and each of them was laced with hard-to-see and dangerous hollows and spurs. There was nothing really to say except "watch it" or "hold tight." We weren't mountain climbers, and this was hard work even for experienced mountaineers. Once I slipped from a plateau over a small ledge and hung there on the rope for a few horrible moments. My friends pulled me to safety, told me to drink water, and then urged me to breathe slowly until I calmed myself.

Occasionally we heard each other gasp or nearly choke from the strong and disturbing scents in the air. Sometimes Emere coughed. But our daring had no voice and we did not speak our fear. We did not cry or scream out when long-eared bats as big as cocker spaniels exited from dark rock shelters just above us. These shelters must have led to deep caves. The bats flew by us now and then, all headed upward, presumably to yet another cave above us.

Then there were the sounds. New sounds. Previously there had been just sloshing sounds or occasionally unpleasant whistles from the canopy, but now there was something different. It was some new menace, of that we were certain. Sometimes the sound was like a thousand pipes; It was reminiscent of the great, tubed monument to Sibelius in Helsinki. This sculpture made the sound of a hundred whistling pipes when the wind blew in from the Baltic Sea at just the right angle.

The thing we heard, however, sometimes sounded like a prehistoric bird, and I thought of *Arthur Gordon Pym* and the cry of "tekeli-li," that enigmatic call Poe described. No one knows where "tekeli-li" came from. Poe's source has never been truly settled. Maybe, I thought giddily in a moment of insanity, we had found it. I truly thought I heard it, just as Lovecraft had his own adventurers hear it in *Mountains of Madness*. It couldn't be, and yet it seemed so. Here, anything seemed possible. I nearly had to slap myself back into reality. Fortunately the "tekeli-li" cry faded away and my imagination took a rest.

After another two or three thousand steps, we began to hear the sounds of scraping movements at a distance above. These scrapes were followed by crashing sounds, as if a forest of trees were falling at the same time, and then a low persistent rumble. How can I describe a sound? It was as if a thousand lions were grumbling at a distance or a great *digeridoo* or a fabulous multi-reed instrument, a *duduk* as large as a tree, trembling and clicking still far above us.

It was not, we could tell, a waterfall, though it had some of that sound quality too.

The crashing came nearer, or we came nearer to it. The earth under our feet began to tremble. It felt almost like an earthquake. And then we saw the source of at least the dizzying movement that unsteadied us. It was a group of wild boars the size of elephants. It is impossible to describe how terrifying they were to see. Their tusks had grown to enormous size, like the tusks of elephants, but curled back onto their brows. They were chasing something, though all of them seemed to be blind, because they ran headlong into the trunks of massive trees, many of which fell over on impact. Each boar, in his or her turn, was temporarily dazed, then got up and began its heedless hunt again. We stood absolutely still to let them pass, though Emere and Anui had their firearms ready. Aban, however, seemed to have disappeared. He was there and then he wasn't. When danger seems to have passed, everyone relaxed and Aban was there again. This was no time to ask what he had done, but I knew then he had powers and skills beyond what I had ever imagined.

We hadn't walked more than a few yards when we began to see human skeletal remains scattered in the scree and wet, boggy ground, almost invisible at first under and amidst bleached bits of stone. We did not at first know what we were looking at. Then, slowly, our eyes adjusted and we saw the horror. These were intact, still-articulated skeletons, and all of them—and we must have counted the sad evidence of twenty or thirty individuals—had dropped in a position that indicated they had been running down the mountain. Their bones were free of flesh and were a startling white from years of exposure. But the bones had not been torn into bits, gnawed at, or carried away by animals. There were even a few scraps of what must have been clothing here and there and some brass buckles and buttons, clearly military issue. In the muck and mire we could make out the moldy, grimy remains of packets of *Gauloises* and *Gitanes* cigarettes. As we searched a more extensive area, we found even a couple of unopened bottles of Armagnac and at least one Courvoisier VSOP Cognac.

Whatever had happened to these people had happened quickly. Their recumbent bones, lying unceremoniously in the morass and stone, did not indicate prolonged writhing or misery. There must have been something they were running from, paroxysmal flight caused by a vision, a sound, a certainty of deadly danger, and then the end. Sudden and complete.

We managed to keep apace in our quest to reach the top in spite of this most unholy specter. However, a bird ran across our path, and I thought Emere would not go forward. The bird, long thought extinct in these islands, was a *kalae,* and it was crying furiously. The sound was always considered an omen of death by the ancient ones, Emere said. It had last been heard, she thought she'd been told, in great numbers, in 1918, just before the population of one whole island was exterminated by a worldwide flu epidemic. This *kalae* was a species of the red-billed rail described by members of the Cook expeditions in the late 1700s. In fact, it looked very much like the *Gallirallus pacificus* painted by Georg Forster who was with Cook. Perhaps this island, though in other ways nearly destroyed by humans, had not had an invasion of the cats and rats that were thought to have killed the *Gallirallus pacificus* on other islands. The bird, you see, could not fly, and was therefore vulnerable to such predators.

It was a dandy looking animal with bright red bill and nape of neck and colorful legs and feet. The specimen that crossed our path had a rakish white stripe over its beady eye. The cry was pathetic and its presence on the path more portentous when it turned sharply and looked directly at us before disappearing again, still crying, into the woods. Where had it come from? Was it never extinct? Or had some trick of the manipulated universe we had entered brought it back? Or was it simply a vision sent to warn us?

Emere stood stalk still. It was as if all the blood had left her body. In fact, her legs began to swell, and she began to swoon. We lay her carefully on the path and raised her feet above her head. We gave her water and talked with her. Aban brought out a little bundle from his knapsack and gave her what appeared to be a bit of betel and lime to chew. He scattered some parched rice, also in his kit, all around her body and brushed us all with a branch he cut from a nearby tree. The bird, now long gone, could still be heard in the distance, but Emere stood up and was determined to continue the journey. Her legs slowly took on their usual shape. Still, she warned us that more danger was certainly ahead. Her grandmother had passed on stories of the *kalae* that appeared just before battles in her time. At least she thought it was a *kalae*. Aban spoke quietly about the horned bills, another omen bird, as portents of evil to come, stories he had learned from an Indonesian or Malaysian grandparent. Still, he did not appear impressed by the incident or in any way frightened.

CHAPTER XXXV

On We Go

The oldest and strongest emotion of mankind is fear.
H.P. Lovecraft

The rumbles and grumbles were louder and the earth trembled slightly as we climbed even higher, so now we knew it was not only wild boars that we had heard. Our rope was a comfort. We glanced at each other frequently, both to share our growing fear and to reassure ourselves that we were in this together. The bonds among us were stronger than the rope.

Vegetation thinned and now we were climbing sheer rock outcroppings, one foot at a time, seeking ledges and footings carefully. Phad was beside himself attempting to find alternative routes. We should have leashed him. The often implacable Phad imprudently, I thought, took a side trail and we lost sight of him completely.

Emere and Anui paused long enough to check their weapons. We signaled each other to move stealthily, keep our heads down, and speak only in whispers. Anui was almost pale. He had told us the night before that he feared meeting spiritual guardians of this hideous place. The mutant animals had awakened old memories, stories his grandparents had told him.

There had been an ancient region where no human dared enter, his grandfather said. There were two keepers lodged there: enormous beings made of rock but animated and able to speak and act when intruders came upon them. They threatened to crush those who ignored them. They did this by falling over on any provocateur that denied their authority and rolling on top of him or her, grinding and crunching until the body was thoroughly mashed. Only spells and enchantment could counter the guardians. Anui thought and thought and asked his dreams to help him.

He was certain that he would need the spells today. He was certain we would meet with opposition in our quest to reach the top.

The stone guardians, his grandfather said, required the sacrifice of a giant boar that was to be cooked and eaten. In the story, a heroic man who wished to enter the sacred place skewered two of these creatures with a long sharp spear. He then slung the spear over his shoulder, boars hanging from it, and made his way home. He was greeted by his terrified family with stacks of baked breadfruit, rambutan, papaya, and perfectly grilled thon or tuna. He threw the boars to the ground, and, after he ate the fruit and fish, began to dig an enormous hole in which to cook the giant boars. The hole was so large it led to the center of the earth where hot molten rocks bubbled and steamed forth. No fire need be built. He lined the hole with trees he cut from the forest, each downed with one blow of his mighty parang, a roughly forged sword that he carried that hung from his waist in a wooden scabbard. It was as long as his leg. He covered the trees with a thousand banana leaves and put the cleaned boars on top. Then he covered the boars with more banana leaves. The boars cooked for six days. Villagers came from all over the island to feast. The hole remained opened and every few years a puff of smoke rises into the air and sometimes the molten rock flushes forth.

After the feast, the hero told his grandfather that he must return for he was now able to pass the guardians.

"But why must you return?" his grandfather asked.

"Because whatever is there must be known. Whatever secrets are held must be revealed. The earth must understand in order for all creatures to live. And this is my job."

"And what do you believe is there?" the grandfather asked.

"The product of wasted genius. The spawn of misguided nations. The detritus of centuries of hate."

"And what do you believe you can do about all of this?"

"I can and will deny its power to shape our lives."

And with that, the hero turned on his heel, armed only with his spear and parang, and climbed the mountain once again.

CHAPTER XXXVI

On the Beach

Only your real friends will tell you when your face is dirty.
Sicilian Proverb

We could not have known how our friends back on the beach fared. Of course, we had signaled them in the morning, and Anui had seen the smoke from their fire and received a mirror-flashed reply to his own signal. Gertrude and Lygia had spent the day before watching for our signals, keeping the fire stoked, and singing and playing together. Gertrude had a fabulous memory and did not really need to write down her poetic chants, but Lygia notated her musical accompaniment. The more they sang and played, the calmer the beach seemed. Roosters stopped crowing, frogs stopped jumping, and, indeed, a wonderful stillness came over the waterfront. The only movements and sounds around their little fireside nest of ground cloths and pillows were caused by the gentle swells from the lagoon splashing against the sandy beach.

As they continued to play and chant and sing, some creatures, all in some way marked by an evolutionary calamity, came close by and seemed to be eerily beguiled by the peculiar women. The rapture was contagious it seemed, for even lagoon fishes came near the shore and some albino dolphins began leaping and passing a misshapen coconut from nose to nose just off shore. The charm of the pair of unlikely friends drew more and more creatures near, and they settled in couples or family groupings on the sand and watched, listened, or fell into deep sleepy swoons.

When the humans tired of singing and playing and telling stories about their lives, Lygia offered to fix Gertrude's hair. It took more than two hours of plucking things out of it to begin the process. Then Lygia retrieved an oak handled brush from her pack and worked carefully to tease out the years of tangle. It was not a pleasant process for either woman, but it was more painful, certainly, for Gertrude. They both bathed, and Lygia scrubbed Gertrude's scalp, hair, and back. Gertrude looked a new person. She had more tattoos than Lygia had previously thought. With the dirt scrubbed away, they stood out distinctly, like masterful etchings against her dark skin. Certainly none of the folks on the mountain, me included, would have recognized her after Lygia's ministrations. She rose like a Venus from the shell-strewn waters as Lygia, her companion *Horae*, held out a clean, hand-painted pareo with which she could cover her body.

Gertrude offered to return the favor by executing a tattoo on Lygia's right shoulder. They decided it should be a traditional, old-style, turtle design. First, she drew the design. It was a smallish turtle, about three inches by two. Then, following the lines of the drawing, she pricked the skin with a needle attached to a springy bit of a stick. She tapped the needle-stick with another, sturdier stick. Then she rubbed bits of finely ground hematite from a lump in her satchel. The hematite colored the turtle a deep red. It was important to keep the tattoo clean and protected until it healed, so Lygia covered it loosely with a bit of plaster and pulled on a tee shirt.

After the tattoo session, Lygia produced a nail kit. Gertrude's toenails were like claws, and they had begun to curl. They did each other's toes, filing and buffing, and thereby executed as complete a pedicure and manicure on each other as they could manage with their limited instruments. They rubbed their feet and hands with coconut oil.

Lygia and Gertrude agreed that they had had a fine day, though not without concern for their companions high on the mountain. The flashes from atop the canopy had come as expected though, so they assumed that all was well with their friends. The agreed upon signal for problems had not been seen.

The creatures that had observed all these curious human rituals returned to their own lairs as the sunset and the moon came up in the west. Gertrude and Lygia had no trouble keeping the fire going, but, even in the bright night, the moon reflected off the lagoon water heightening the effect, they needed lanterns for their own after dark plans. With the help of the added illumination, they fixed a hearty meal of corned beef, fried in an iron skillet over our back up Primus stove. Into the beef they chopped birds eye chili peppers and scallions and then added several dashes of soy sauce. In a separate skillet, they diced and fried two white potatoes with a red onion. When those dishes were complete, they poached two eggs for exactly three minutes. Each made a banana leaf plate and served up the corned beef topped with an egg. Gertrude needed more hot sauce on hers.

The animals who had been their companions during the day stayed respectfully away even though they must have smelled the food. However, the mosquitoes were not so kind. Gertrude and Lygia ensconced themselves under the giant net we'd left behind.

They had never seen mosquitoes so large. They were nearly the size of bumblebees.

As they settled in for the long evening, they thought of their friends and wondered how they fared. Then they took a plank from the big canoe, found the Mexican Train set in the cargo hold, and played a game that really was not very satisfying for only two. The game got sillier after they each had a couple of gin and tonics. Gertrude was declared the winner, though they stayed awake only long enough to reach the double six. Gertrude brought out the bottle of coconut oil again. They rubbed each other's feet once more, giggling all the while, and then fell asleep.

The next morning, they saw Anui's signal from above and rejoiced. All was well.

Gertrude began immediately composing the next chapter of her ever-growing story of the trip.

Oh, sight unseen they sallied forth.
With all our hopes, they set their course.
Their courage, flamed with flair and dash,
We knew lived on: we saw their flash.

What demons, what soul-wrenching fiends,
Might come to check these human beings?
What twisted gene pools might emerge?
What ogres of the night converge?

What will they see, what horrors wait?
Will we be privy to their fate?
Or will their travels be benign?
All day we'll watch to see their sign.

Be well our friends, we sing for thee
And send our spells to keep you free.

CHAPTER XXXVII

The Hole in the Center of the Earth

Schrödinger's Cat Walked into a Bar...and Then He Didn't

We saw a flattened cone of a volcanic crater in the distance. The foot of the final peak was looming before us. The scoria became rougher, and, finally, the rocks we climbed, all covered with a sloughing, gelatinous substances, gave way to a slick, glassy volcanic rock, black as jet and smooth as obsidian. It took effort and balance to move ahead on this difficult, slippery surface. We often found ourselves sliding backwards, but we made slow and steady progress nevertheless. The rumble beneath our feet continued, as did the uncanny whistling and the low growling sound. And even from this distance we could also hear the roar of the waves in the sea below.

I walked on a few feet ahead of my friends. We were still roped, and, though I felt reassured by this, I was grateful to find some vesicles or cavities in the igneous rock into which I could put at least a toe. Occasionally I managed to work my hand into an under cling.

Weapons were at ready. Emere, Aban, and Anui were hyperalert, eyes fixed straight ahead. But this was my work. No weapon on earth could settle whatever account was owed. The messages from the spirit had led us to this place to settle a debt for all of humanity.

Then, mounted on a glassy black peak of this sheer and shiny incline, on a ridge above us, apparently settled into the caldera of the volcano, I saw it. Beyond the feathered nut pines was its lair. I had to climb along a rock edge, a precipitous drop to my right, to reach it. I wanted to recoil from its visage, but could not. In fact, I found adrenaline racing through my body and a kind of embarrassing thrill as I braced myself for what would happen next. This was a state I always welcomed. It was a rapture that made all else in the world drop away, and it seemed only to come to me when I put myself in situations of risk. In that state, time stands still or is non-existent. I am at once super keen and know exactly what to do and am not encumbered by logic or analysis. Some people call it the "flow."

Nevertheless, and in spite of my ecstatic state, I knew that whatever this thing was, it must be challenged, I must be ready, and I must be sensible in the truest sense of the word.

The thing was all pumped up like a Peking Duck that's been inflated with water like a balloon to separate skin from meat. Only we sure were not going to eat this creature. As I approached it, almost slithering on my hands and knees now, something like a jaw shot forward from under a mouth-like shape. The jaw seemed to bow and amorphous limbs to genuflect before me as if I were a goddess. The jaw dragged along the ground and sparse vegetation before me, plowing a grotesque path almost to my feet.

I reminded myself of what an old Australian doubles tennis partner, Beverly, had taught me to do in these times: "Just close your eyes and think of England, dearie." So I did. I started singing a verse of Jerusalem. William Blake's stirring words would surely give me courage:

Bring me my Bow of burning gold;
Bring me my Arrows of desire:
Bring me my Spear: O clouds unfold!
Bring me my Chariot of fire!

A scene from the film *Merry Christmas, Mr. Lawrence* marched, illogically, through my memory as I sang and faced the beast. I was ready.

The thing. Its "mouth"—or was it a pseudo foot? For it seemed to be a thing that could propel the whole mass forward inch by inch—was like a giant labia with many flaps and folds each in the shape of a *vesica pisces*, at least six feet long and three or four feet wide. It spewed a blood-like, though translucent, substance as it opened and closed. Now and then, it vented steamy breath that smelled like a combination of rotted fish and an overflowing pit latrine. When it vented, it revealed great sharp teeth set in several rows both above and below. Gauzy drops of the blood came toward me and spattered around my feet and onto my face and clothes. A splayed "tongue" shot out now and then, pink and covered with spidery webbed purple veins. All around it a steamy substance belched and smoked, and from beneath the head-like bubble above the mouth sprouted countless tentacles, each writhing and trembling and each at least twelve feet in length. They were smooth and spotted on top but covered underneath with jagged sucker like smaller mouths or nipples. I could see now that the creature was seated inside an opening in the mountain, something made, it seemed, by human tools, for there were chiseled marks all around the edge of the hole as if made by hammers or gigantic drills. I deduced that the dead soldiers had been sent to place an atomic charge in this place to test an underground nuclear weapon and that something had gone terribly wrong.

My cargo pants were covered with the blood now and my booted feet were sliding in the slime of the creature's discharges. Somewhere deep in the head, barely visible, were baleful eyes set in deep, boney sockets. Evil seeming as they were, still they seemed almost to beg for pity. My companions gathered behind me and clung breathlessly to the almost vertical, slick rock.

They uttered nothing sensible. Or useful.

Anui said something like, "Fuck it." Helpful.

Emere said, "Ah shit." Also helpful.

Only Aban seemed still on top of the situation. He was rigid, his arms rose in a seeming prayer or salute. I could see his lips moving ever so slightly.

Just as I thought it couldn't get worse, a giant slimy sack shot out of the mouth of the creature. It turned itself inside out and covered the "face" of the creature entirely in a fresh layer of nacreous slime before it withdrew again. It was as if the whole had received a fresh coat of paint, for it glistened and glowed with rainbow colors in the sunlight. As the stomach pouch withdrew, a cloud of flying ants the size of puppies swarmed over it and attached themselves to the new slime coating. They sucked at the beast whose frantic tentacles had no effect upon them. From out of the jungle, triple-headed snakes of many colors crawled, also apparently attracted by the slime. Once the creature was covered with these parasites, the stomach shot out again, covered all the newcomers, and carried them quickly away, presumably into the animal's interior where they would be digested.

Just as the stomach or whatever organ it might have been had withdrawn completely, Phad appeared behind the beast and commenced a horrible baying. He was a headstrong, courageous animal, and sometimes made horrible choices in order to demonstrate his gutsiness. This was one of those bad choices.

I looked back at my friends. They stood glassy-eyed like a row of dead mullets.

"We're for it," I yelled at them. "Stay with me." I thought of Beverly again. "Well old girl, " she used to say to me when we were losing a match, "we're up against it this time, and no mistake."

If we were exhausted, as I was at that moment, she'd yell, "we've paid out nearly every stiver we've got," a stiver being an old Dutch nickel, "but we'll get our selves out of this fix. We always do." Well, I'd soon be out of stivers and I was still in a fix.

Phad, too, was really properly in the soup and I was afraid he'd catch it for sure this time. We saw that his feet were caught up in the slime and he was unable to move away. He struggled but became more gummed up as he did. His eyes were full of fear, and we were all dreading the worst for him. We feared the stomach would shoot out again. We tried to signal Phad to drop and quiet himself. This he attempted, though clearly all his instincts told him to do otherwise.

The creature didn't really move at all then. It seemed not to notice Phad. It did continue to writhe and smack its hideous lips and was still emitting a deep grumbling sound that grew louder and louder. It was so loud now that I slithered just a bit further back.

Still, the creature made no move to envelop Phad, so we stayed put too. The grumble turned to a loud piercing cry. I held my hands over my ears and literally was immobilized with the pain that found its way deep into my head. I found bits of cotton tissue in my pockets and stuffed them into my ears. I pulled the bandana off my neck and quickly tied it around my head, over my ears. I could still hear the creature, but it was now muffled enough that I could not feel the deep pain. The others were there behind me waiting for my signal. What were we to do? The fat was certainly in the fire.

I reckoned that it was time to get my wind up and consult my spirit guides. I had followed their instructions. We had prepared ourselves, traveled for days, met with the misshapen, hideous results of human insanity, climbed to the source. But now what?

This was not the *Island of Dr. Moreau*. This was not regression or devolution. This was a land destroyed by the knowing act of human beings who wanted to test their bombs and understand the consequences of the fallout from them. They were willing to use beautiful, innocent animals, fruits, vegetables, trees, and even human beings as their guinea pigs. Those who made the decision to use this island and many others for their tests still walked free upon the planet. No jury had convicted them. No crime had been alleged. No world court or United Nations had held them accountable. And most of the world would never know or see what their cruel, unforgivable acts had wrought. Whole villages had been abandoned. Whole families, generations of families, had fled. Whole islands had been rendered unlivable. And here we were, face to face, with the embodiment of those evil deeds.

CHAPTER XXXVIII

Overcoming the Monster: Healing the Earth

A Not Insignificant Undertaking today. We've done what we were sent to do. I don't know how long our fix is good for, but at least we've done something.
From the journals of Fiona Elizabeth Kelly

Spirit guide? What? Am I crazy? Here I was, hanging by my fingernails, so to speak, my heart in my boots, sweating in my suddenly unwicking socks, and beset by a demon with a monstrous scudding jaw. I was floundering, lurching here and there, as I tried to find and keep my footing, and lashed to a team of friends who had followed me with alacrity and stuck with the mission regardless of the risks. My dear dog companion was stuck and helpless, at the mercy of a hellish being. And I thought I had the luxury of consulting my "spirits?" Hadn't they got me here? Wasn't I asking a question for which I knew the answer? Action was needed. I'd not be showing a white feather. None of us would.

One quick gesture to Emere and she grabbed the flares out of her rucksack, not a bit of a jitter in her hands, and positioned four of them on the flat of a slim black rock ledge, lit a match, and touched the wicks. The flares rose high into the sky and created color, light, and left a dandy condensation trail behind. There was no doubt that Gertrude and Lygia would see and read the signal. They'd know we were in some kind of combat but not asking for help. Yet. I made a second gesture to Anui, and he raised his pistol, ready to pull the trigger. Another gesture to Aban…but he had no weapon, of course. Still, he looked awfully pulled together. What would he do?

I hadn't needed to gesture to Aban. He had moved into a statue like posture, two hands poised as if to strike, his left leg flexed and foot arched as if ready to kick. At first it looked to me like a Tai Chi posture. Then I recognized it. Silat. He had studied silat. The red bandana, the ability to disappear. It all made sense now. He was a silat master, a mystical fighter, a Sufi, and a well-trained genius of the martial arts. He had never lost his grip. And he was ready now to go to work.

Silat is an ancient discipline that combines a repertoire of ancient Southeast Asian gestures with deep meditation. Silat can be used effectively in hand-to-hand combat. It draws upon both the Chinese and Indian "soft" forms of martial arts. Some of the moves come from the close observation of fighting cocks and other animals. The ancient ones had no arms or armor. They learned to use their bodies and their ability to induce mass hallucinations when encountering the enemy. Of course, some would say what masters can bring forth and make manifest are not hallucinations at all, but the substantiation of centuries of spirit helper combatants who will come to the aid of those fighting a just cause.

Aban's initial stance seemed to draw the attention of the sluggish being in the vast crater. Its eyes rested on his form. Aban began, then, with a salute, a salute I knew was directed to his own teacher and the teacher of teachers from whom his art descended. Then he began moving quickly, stepping and kicking and moving his arms with the precision of a ballet dancer. His body moved faster and his chops and punches, though seemingly at the air, became more forceful. Then, in a whir, he became a hundred and then a thousand. There were then, on that mountainside a mass of men and women, all with red bandanas round their foreheads and all moving at once. I could see them. We all could see them.

They performed beautifully; they executed perfect, unison, kicks and crouches, punches and crawls. The air around us moved as quickly as did they. A great wind engulfed us all as their energy subdued all others'. Phad was picked up by it and shot through the air over our heads and cleared from danger. Emere stood near me, bent to grasp my shoulders from behind, and dropped her musket to her side. I stood up with Emere, but found my knees were shaking uncontrollably. We held each other tight so as not to be swept up in near hurricane that engulfed us all. Anui took several steps back and then fell to his knees in wonder. He lowered his pistol.

I had heard about the power of silat after it was used in 1969 in Kuala Lumpur during Chinese-Malay confrontations. I didn't know until this moment that what I'd heard had really happened. That use of silat in 1969 resulted in many deaths. We all knew, together, that our own turn to violence could not surmount the evil we had come to counter. Our will had to deny power to it, and that denial meant asserting our commitment to a greater strength. Aban was showing us the way.

Over the roar of the hurricane and the rumble of the earth beneath us, we heard a mighty soprano voice singing. It was a soaring song, with words set to a tune that sounded suspiciously like Mussorgsky's *Night on Bald Mountain*. The voice followed the melody line but added thirds, fifths, sevenths, elevenths and overtones where none were called for by the composer. It was Gertrude's voice coming from the beach and calling on all her spiritual resources to help us. The energy from the silat dancers followed the excitement of the music. Gertrude's voice echoed round and round so that it seemed a chorus of hundreds. Then we could hear strains of a cello. The movements and the voices churned the air at such a fantastic velocity that we were all caught up in a frenzy of emotions. If the beast had a true brain, it would have been scrambled in the midst of in all this drama. And perhaps that's just what happened.

It was the silat that saved the day. And Gertrude and Lygia's music…the music that went on and on.

CHAPTER XXXIX

Meanwhile, Back on the Beach

The Amazing Manifestation of Dame Kiri Te Kanawa's Voice

Lygia was playing so quickly and vigorously that her cello was visibly vibrating. Indeed, even a few chips of varnish were dashed from the neck of the instrument where her fingers pressed to produce an excruciatingly beautiful tremolo. Shortish, damp strands of blonde hair flew across her face, whipping it unmercifully. Gertrude was suddenly blessed with a range far beyond that she had used for her normal chanting and shanties. She was channeling Dame Kiri Te Kanawa through an ancient portal that her prayers opened and led her to Dame Kiri's Maori ancestors. Lygia and Gertrude were prepared for their work. Their ecstatic state was fueled by the urgent desire to save us and put back into place whatever grim horrors had been leaking forth from this island and disturbing the spirits of Moa Nui and the other peoples in the region. The quick-witted women played with all the intensity they could muster and their music pierced the dense jungle, rose above the roaring of the waves at the reef's edge, and swept sharply up to the mountain top.

The women sent up their blessings on the wings of the best weapons they had.

The animals who occupied the shore area and who had learned to love Gertrude and Lygia, crept silently away into the jungle as the music ended. Nothing could be done for these guiltless victims of the worst that humankind has to offer. They would live on, perhaps without issue, perhaps suffering hideous deaths from disease caused by radiation, or perhaps bearing others of their kind that mock the original beauty and vitality of their species. But they would have now the memory of something good coming from a human contact. They would have the memory of the fabulous, healing music Gertrude and Lygia made that day.

CHAPTER XXXX

From Evil, Beauty

When all's said and done, all roads lead to the same end. So it's not so much which road you take, as how you take it.
Charles de Lint

The air was suddenly still. Emere and I looked around us in a daze. She slowly lowered herself to her knees. I couldn't stand on my shaking pins anymore either. I threw myself full length on the edge of a slick precipice to my side. I found a toehold. There was a thick vein of scoria just below. I managed to get my other foot into one of the rough crevices where roots had made their way through tiny cracks in this ample basaltic river of ancient lava. The roots had pushed the rock layers slightly askew. Enough to make a place for me to put some weight. That firm perch, toes gripping ancient fissures, helped me feel that I was fairly safe. I watched as Emere moved down to the surface from a crouching position and then crawl on her hands and knees toward a scraggly tree. She got close enough to grasp at a limb. Anui was tucked sideways into a barrow-shaped lava tube that extended from a narrow but sturdy ledge. Aban still stood above me and held a calm, meditative pose in spite of all that had transpired around him. I could still see the hundreds of warriors he had summoned, but they were becoming dream-like, hazy, and then transparent. In a few moments, they were gone.

There was an enormous chasm below me, but the way back down the mountain was clear. While the wind and music swirled around me, I noticed the creature in the crater. The wet parts seemed to be withdrawing. There were no more eyes. The slime was shrinking back into the crater, beneath the creature. It was a slow process, but I was certain that it was losing its awful power before our eyes. A dried substance, something like dried and wrinkled snakeskin, was left on the rock surface in its wake. As the wind and a faint melody continued, the earth trembled and groaned beneath and around us. There seemed no menace now. And then, without warning, all was quiet.

Aban stood alone. Anui came out of his barrow. Emere let go the branch and moved along the obsidian, crawling carefully on her stomach, and came up to my side. There was no need for conversation. We just looked around in wonder.

We saw together that what was left on the crater, fully plugging the entire cavity, was a gigantic cowrie shell. The egg-like mound was upright. Indeed, it was a most beautiful shell. We took it to be what was known as the snake-head cowrie *Cypraea Caputserpentis*. It was brown and speckled with brilliant white along its top. The stunning, glassy exterior shone and glistened where the sun glanced off its bulging crown. It almost begged to be touched, so inviting and glorious was its appearance. We realized that the lobes of the creature's mantle had covered the shell, and what we had witnessed as a horror were the maneuvers and manipulations that the mantle, the living cowrie, had made in an attempt to find food. The mantle's many extensions and protuberances had grown to gross proportions due to extremes of habitat degradation and the effect of radiation on its molecular structure. It was, after all, only a large snail, and it too had been victimized.

Some soldier had probably collected a pocketful of shells while on the beach. Perhaps he had thought them beautiful and had planned to make a necklace or bracelet of them for a loved one back home. Certainly, at least one of these cowries had not been not dead and the soldier had inadvertently carried the doomed snail up the mountain, away from its home in the sea. Then, when the explosion came, the creature was subjected to intense radiation and somehow managed to live on in the horror of its new home on the mountain, adding daily to its girth and becoming what we had seen upon our arrival.

The shell now thoroughly and finally plugged the hole, from which radiation and dangerous radiated waters had continued to leak after all these years. The creature and the dangers had lost their powers over this little island. The spirits had lead us to heal at least this small bit of the planet, one that left unchecked in its degradation could spoil fish and fowl in the miles and miles of ocean that circulated around it.

CHAPTER XXXXI

Gertrude Rejoices

Gertrude, though still humming loudly, could sense the shift. She could feel the work was finished. She threw back her head, looked up to the mountain top where Anui was almost visible high in the canopy from where he sent the mirror message: "Mission accomplished. All safe." She grabbed Lygia and gave her a big hug. The women rejoiced. The flashes told her that their friends were on their way down the mountain. She began to sing:

We're bold as rocks; we breathe and move together.
We're strong as stone; we sing away our fear.
We've followed many stars and constellations.
We've climbed the very highest belvedere.

And from that austere height we launched our mission,
And we have done what we were sent to do.

And yet we'd like to live a life more peaceful.
We'd rather dance together through the night
And not mop up mistakes of thieves and cowards
And suffer those we'd all like to indict...

For heedless acts of arrogance and greed,
And deeds that jeopardize our children's lives,
We'd like to bring them all to trial and damn them
And make a world where everyone can thrive.

A righteous act will never go unnoticed.
Make loving gestures everywhere you dare.
Do what is right; don't waste your time on anger,
And lead the march with flowers in your hair.

Sail through the waters, navigate with gusto.
Sail on with stories of our jaunty quest.
Sail through the jewel of misty sun light.
Sail through the hefty currents, mount the crests.

Though Lygia thought Gertrude might need a rest, she continued to humor her and her versifying. She suggested, however, that they might dance together to celebrate and channel their emotions. The women stripped off the few clothes they were wearing. They smeared ochre from Gertrude's satchel on their faces, put feathers that had drifted in from the sea in their hair, covered their most private parts with seaweed clusters, and began to dance a ferocious dance. Their ample bosoms and buttocks bounced happily as they beat a deep channel in the sand. Their animal friends came back from the jungle to watch. They'd been, used to a calmer spirit in the women. They dropped back for a bit when they saw the romping, and then came shyly forward. This was something else they would never forget. Humans. How very peculiar and confusing they are.

After the dance, Gertrude apologized to Lygia for her last song and the use of the word "belvedere," then. She knew she had been tired, overwrought, and forcing her rhymes. Furthermore, it wasn't like her, she said, to be blatantly corny or preachy. This song was, she admitted, both. But right now she didn't care. Neither did Lygia. It was all part of the journey.

CHAPTER XXXXII

Back to Our Friends

Luckily, just before night, all four of us had lashed ourselves firmly to the fragments of the windlass, lying in this manner as flat upon the deck as possible. This precaution alone saved us from destruction.
Narrative of A. Gordon Pym by Edgar Allen Poe

I was standing now, just below the obsidian shelf. Both of my feet were on terra firma. My friends were safe, and the volcano was plugged, at least for now. I looked up. The sky was clear and blue overhead. I could see the sun from my perch. I could see birds high over head. I hadn't noticed before; I had been focused on the horror of that crawling mantle.

Though my heart was still beating too fast, and I was bloody and filthy, I wanted to sing. I thought about one of the Canadian singer Jane Siberry's lyrics. How did it go? Something like seeing something unbelievable, something grand. It was a relief to be thinking about these words and humming the tune, and I found myself smiling. Soon, I was breathing normally again. In fact, I hadn't realized it but I had been sort of holding my breath for several minutes. After a few seconds, I realized it was not just my knees shaking. I was shaking all over, and, though I was happy, I started to cry. And then I sang outloud.

Phad. Where the heck was he? The last I'd seen, he was flying through the air. I whistled. He came to me then, daggled by mud and secretions of the *Cypraea Caputserpentis*. He was filthy, yet fully alive and wagging his whole body. As the dog nuzzled each of us, we eased ourselves back down from the shelf and onto even safer turf and less hazardous footing.

Phad did not let up with his happy yelping and woofs. He was, however, uncomfortable and kept trying to scratch his body with one of his hind legs. Occasionally he rolled on the ground, which made matters worse. His fur was sticky from his encounter with the mantle and he was bristling all about with burrs and seedpods and things we certainly didn't want to take off the island with us. When we got a bit further down the mountain, we tried to clean him with water from our bottles. We picked and pulled at him.

When he began to whimper and try to pull away, we thought he was tired of our plucking. We tried to reassure him and relax him so we could finish working on his coat, but he continued to lunge out of our grasp and finally managed to pull away altogether. We whistled and called for him to come back. It was no use. He bounded off into the jungle a little ways, then came back and looked at us, then went deeper into the trees. He did this repeatedly. He clearly wanted us to follow. Indeed, his eyes flashed and his ears and tail moved in ways that gave us a clear sense of what he required of us. Follow, follow. There was no doubt. And even though Phad sometimes made mistakes in his enthusiasm and desire to serve, he usually had pretty good instincts, so we gave up trying to persuade him to come back to us and went along.

He gave a long glance over his shoulder often, assuring himself that we were with him. He was eager but slowed enough for us to get down the slippery slope, past the scraggy vegetation, and into the dense jungle. We had to chop and snick and snee to get through the succulent hanging vines, and the deep green, luxuriant ferns. It was dark and quite hard to see now that we were under the canopy again. What sky we could see above was grey and somehow menacing now, as if clouds obscured the sun. A storm had moved in, and it had happened fast. This was not a good sign—not during this cyclone season.

"This better be worth it," Emere said. She was aware that we were losing time and this could be dangerous with the possibility of an impending squall. Finally, Phad came to a halt and stood, doing his best imitation of a point. There, deep in a well-hidden bower, was a pair of *kalae* birds and a nest with two perfect eggs.

The eggs were large, much larger than one would expect given the size of the birds. We could see now that the *kalae* was larger than a chicken, and, in fact, looked like a big chicken. It was probably at least a foot and a half tall from foot to crest. We decided that they were probably in the same family as the extinct kiwi of New Zealand. Though flightless, we had observed that they could run very fast, like the ostrich.

Emere seemed at ease in their presence. Whatever danger she had feared had passed and the birds seemed at peace as well.

There seemed very little difference in the appearance of the two birds, but they were clearly a mating pair. If they were in the ostrich family, we assumed this pair was a monogamous couple. One was a bit larger and it, the one we presumed to be the male, was guarding the nest and eggs. We realized that it had removed itself from the eggs to face us, and, when we made no gestures it deemed threatening, it sat again upon the nest. Though the birds were cowering and trembling all over, the male had returned to take care of the eggs and the female stood steadfastly near him. What brave and humble birds! Though, of course, it was this very meekness that had gotten birds like them eaten to extinction.

We could not leave the pair here. They were probably not the only *kalae* on the island, but this pair could mean the return of a lost species. We whispered together and began to devise a large basket of fern and palm leaves in which we could fit the nest and birds and carry them down the mountain and back to Moa Nui. It was almost as if the *kalae* understood our intentions. They were easily mollified and consented to be swaddled and lifted from their place.

The birds were safe and so were we. Phad now was prepared to allow us to continue removing the gummy substance and the adhering bits of twigs and vegetation from his body. We would give him another bath in the seawater when we reached the beach, and we would do the same ourselves. We would need to wash all of our clothes, our shoes and boots, and our socks. We could carry nothing back that might sprout or contaminate Moa Nui in any other way. This concern meant that the *kalae* would be quarantined for a time when we got home, given a new diet, and new nesting materials from Moa Nui forests. All of their excrement and their accustomed twigs and grasses would be destroyed. We would pack in a few clams for them to enjoy during the trip. And, of course, we would provide them with clean fresh water.

The rest of the trek down the mountain side was relatively easy. We were at peace with the island and with each other. Phad went ahead of us, no doubt looking forward to a bowl of kibble and reunion with Gertrude and Lygia. He was no worse for the wear. Neither were we.

Gertrude and Lygia spotted us even before we emerged all the way from the dark of the jungle. They rushed forward and embraced us all. We hardly recognized Gertrude, so remarkable and complete was her transformation. There was a tumble of words and laughter as we all lost our balances and fell in each other's arms onto the sand. Phad jumped on top of the heap and nipped and barked in time with our shouts and giggles.

As soon as we all stopped tussling and hooting together, Gertrude insisted that we all take off our clothes and jump into the seawater. We didn't have to be asked twice. We scrubbed each other head to foot. We used natural soaps and bits of sponge we had packed for just this purpose. Then we worked over our clothing. Some of it would be left behind, and burned on the beach. Shoes and boots were tossed into the salt water and brushed thoroughly. We wanted to take no debris or contaminants, biological or not, with us from this place.

The animals that had come to know Gertrude and Lygia watched with curiosity. "More odd human activity," they must have thought. The *kalae* were safely tucked into a clean compartment on the canoe, contained within a box that would not allow even a shred of the nest to drift into the rest of the vessel.

Meanwhile, the sky grew darker though it was early afternoon. We knew the barometric pressure was dropping. We had to leave soon even so. We wanted to leave. We wanted to go home.

Gertrude sang a farewell blessing to the creatures and the island. She found some herbs in her pouch. Then she used the last of the smoldering logs on the fire to set them ablaze. She blew out the flame, and watched till the herbs began to set off a dense smoke. Then she smudged each of us, including Phad, and both canoes. Aban would be returning to his own island and quietly made preparations. He moved quietly and said little. We said a farewell to him and he was off for home. We wondered if we'd hear of him again.

Gertrude sang while Lygia bowed accompaniment before she wrapped her cello for the trip back to Moa Nui.

Winds, blow us home
Storms bless our day
Whales lend your eyes
Moon light our way

Mist be our friend
Waves rise and fall
No harm beset
Friends, hear our call.

She then turned and blessed all the creatures that would continue their odd lives on this poor little dot of land in the South Pacific. We knew that new generations would come, new animals and plants would drift in, and there would be, at least for now, no new pollutants to spoil things further or send disasters out on the currents.

The sky was threatening, but the seas were relatively calm as we steered our way toward Moa Nui. We looked forward to a placid journey home, and began to relax. We also began to think about having a nice evening meal. Emere helped me get my fishing rod ready. I threaded an attractive, octopus-skirt lure on to my line. That sparkly lure was designed to snag a tuna. Gertrude began shredding a coconut so we could marinate my catch. We still had a few breadfruit, so Lygia stoked a fire and prepared to bake one. Anui was, of course, in charge of the canoe. He had checked all the cordage and seams before we left. He had a sail up and was watching it closely.

Meanwhile, back home, what we could not have known was that a cyclone had formed between our position and Moa Nui. It was predicted to slam our island destination within twenty-four hours. Schools were closed and inland emergency shelters were being designated, for the fear was that a strong storm surge would bring flooding in over the reef and lagoon and many homes. People were being evacuated from low-lying areas.

The winds around us had begun to increase in intensity. Even without knowing what was happening at home, we knew we were in trouble. I pulled in my line and we put out the fire. We passed bananas around and ate two or three each. We still had a stash of other snacks and plenty of fresh water. We all made sure that everything was secure on board, and Anui took down the sail. Nobody was panicked, but we knew were in for a ride.

As the winds increased, Anui kept a good eye on direction. Now we couldn't see the sun at all and the dark was coming on us fast. With the cloud cover, we wouldn't see stars or planets. That would mean flying blind. Anui had done it before. Centuries of South Sea navigators had faced these challenges. And, of course, we still had the backup GPS and Gertrude's chants, though if she could not see landmasses and if the currents were whipped up by stormy wave action, she wouldn't be much help.

The wind was stronger by the minute and the waves were enormous. There were great chasms between the waves. The boat fell into these with frightening, bone-jarring crashes. Waves broke over us, nearly swamping us several times, but the boat held up. Because of its design, water poured out the back with every wave we mounted. Finally, we decided to throw ourselves supine on the bottom planks of the canoe. We couldn't hear each other now so Anui brandished thick cords and showed us that he wanted us to lash ourselves onto the boards. We all did this.

We always had a safety line on Phad, but now I tied him down with me and held him tight. He moaned a little and trembled with fear. Once, I almost fell asleep, and the dog made what would have been a fatal leap. Phad was so miserable that he thought to escape the dizzying boat ride, but he would have surely been swept away in the angry sea had he not been attached to me by a rope snugged firmly to his collar. I had to literally fish him in by pulling the rope and grabbing his tail as soon as it emerged from the brine. He didn't try that trick again.

I understood his frustration. It was a hellish night as we rode the bucking canoe and felt the giant waves breaking and spraying all night long. As dawn broke, something changed. Unbeknownst to us, the eye of the cyclone had changed course and the island was spared. At home, people began moving back into their homes, stopping to buy baguettes along the way.

We loosened our ropes and looked about, first at each other and then at the canoe itself. We were so tired that what we first saw were the droopiest, bedraggled people we had ever seen. Us! Anui had stayed upright, bound to the mast, and was completely exhausted. He had a light, scraggly beard. Lygia's hair was flat on her head. Emere's eyes were swollen and had bags under them.

But we were safe and Anui was positive he knew where we were. It was hard to imagine, but he was absolutely certain. He reattached the woven mat sail, rechecked his compass, and assured us that we were on course. The outrigger, or *ama*, was barely hanging on to the *'iako*, or hull, of the canoe. Its struts had been fairly badly battered. However, we had followed the instructions of old timers when we rigged the canoe before we left. We had lashed these with many turns and twists that did not allow the cordage to unravel all together, even though severely tested in extremely choppy waters. We got to work doing what repair work we could given the still fairly heavy seas. The waves were tall enough to douse us every few minutes.

We checked our birds. Fortunately, their carefully protected bundle of nesting materials, wrapped over and over with banana leaves from our home supply, had been stowed and secured, deep into the front of the boat under a large plank. The birds were cosseted deep inside the package. They were fine.

The seas became calmer and the sun came out after an hour or two. A beautiful, large sea turtle swam by us, very near the canoe. It had a hibiscus in its mouth. We took this as a sign. We were safe. We were on our way home. Still, we had another night out and hoped out loud that the excitement was over.

CHAPTER XXXXIII

The Return

Evidence of our Success Precede Us

I think we are home free. The sky is beautiful. I'm seeing lovely, sleek, healthy dolphins. I can't stop grinning and humming L'Amour from Carmen. How love is like a bird. I'm a real romantic at heart, but what gets me going is days like this and great adventures. I'll stop humming soon. I know this can be irritating to my friends.
From the Personal Journal of Fiona Elizabeth Kelly

We were all dog-tired, but alive, keen, and happy when we saw Moa Nui in the distance. It was morning, just after sunrise, and we still had a way to go, but we would be there in maybe three hours. The wind was steady but not excessively exuberant. The sky was a bright blue. Sea birds seemed to be coming out to greet and guide us. A few dolphins jumped and sparkled to our port side. The only clouds we saw marked land masses, one of which we were heading for as quickly as the breeze and sea would let us travel.

Believe it or not, we decided to tidy up. I was just too ragged looking, and so was everyone else. Of course, we had cleansed ourselves thoroughly before leaving Mauntaerae, but now, after a night like the one we'd put in, we were salty and ravaged by the winds. We couldn't do much, but I suggested there might be photographs made upon our landing. That was the motivation we all needed. We dug around in our bags and did a bit of brushing and spiffing. Coconut oil was passed around and lathered on bodies. Hair was brushed or picked. I tied a bandana around my head to keep my hair from looking too wild. Then I cleaned my sunglasses and dug around for my toothbrush.

We each had our little fears. Gertrude was nervous about appearing too normal. Lygia feared there would be too many people. She petted her cello, which was back, since the beginning of our return, in its giant plastic bag. Phad tried to pace. He knew we were getting close to home. He wondered if the pig would have been eaten in his absence. He dearly hoped so. Anui got a razor out of his pack and tried unsuccessfully to remove the fuzz on his face. He managed to nick himself early in the process and stopped.

We made certain that everything was properly stowed and returned to its place. We had some breakfast, gave Phad some kibble and fresh water, checked the birds, and then stashed all our garbage and food. We did a little more work on the outrigger. It was easier to make repairs in these seas.

There were spotters on the quay. It turns out, in spite of their troubles with the cyclone, we had not been forgotten. People had been praying, singing, and sending blessings to us. Those who had been appointed to watch for us sent runners throughout the island as soon as they saw us on the horizon. By the time we were ready to enter the lagoon, around eleven, a fleet of the *La république de Moa Nui* outriggers had been launched. It was the national racing team! They were dressed in bright red, green, and black—the colors of the island's flag. They were a beautiful sight as they sped like arrows toward us.

We could see people, all the people of the island, gathering on the quay and we could hear singing. Large flags and banners of welcome were waving in the light breeze. Our outrigger escorts tossed flowers to us even as we were still in the process of landing. People on the quay mobbed our canoe as we came onto the beach. Each of us was almost instantly bear-hugged from left and right and gleefully lifted out of the canoe. People laughed and kissed us as they eagerly stood for a turn to hang shell necklaces and flowers around our necks. The hugging and kissing was relentless. It was a mosh pit I didn't seek to escape, so sweet was the touch of and smell of all our eager greeters.

Eventually the initial enthusiasm of the welcome committee waned. Even so, all through the rest of my time on Moa Nui,

I could expect to receive lovely salutations and sweet, damp kisses on my sunburned cheeks. As we left the beach, a band of ukuleles players encircled us and began to play while the children's choir sang and marched with us. We were then escorted toward the large grassy park in the middle of Besoin. People had to embrace and steady us, for we were wobbly and very tired. Our bodies and minds were finally relaxing and, as they did, we began to feel the consequences of the days of tension and exertion. We all felt aches and pains and found a profusion of bruises and scratches.

Several portable tents had been set up in the park and under these were what seemed like acres of tables. On the tables there was a display of food. People were ready to feast and party. Not only were people happy to see us home safely, but also they were delighted that the full strength of the cyclone had missed Moa Nui, and they were happy that we had met with success. They didn't ask us—they knew. Something had lifted. Everyone had felt it. There had been no new reports of odd happenings for three days. The time of menstruation had come and only those who might expect to bleed under normal circumstances were bleeding. No clothes had been taken from drawers and arranged on the floor. Missionaries were able to remember their purpose, but, to the delight of many, had decided to abandon it. Things were back, the islanders said, to almost normal.

Lygia, who had no doubt long since been reported missing off the coast of the Big Island in Hawaii, asked to get to someone's computer or phone so that she could Skype or call her family in Fogo. The mayor of the town took her directly to his office and served her tea while she explained to worried aunties in Newfoundland that she was indeed alive and well. The lines suddenly went dead just as she was getting to the juicy parts. This was not a mysterious event. It happened all the time.

"But never mind," the mayor said. "I'll take care of this."

So he took her to the beach, put her into the backbench of his little open kayak, and rowed her to a friend's sailboat. There she was patched in to an open line via the radio on the boat.

Meanwhile, the rest of us were ushered under the tents in the park. More groups of musicians were playing island favorites on guitars. A few people had conga drums. There were some dancers from the dance troupe. Near the tent, on the beach, a giant pit contained a very healthy and very large pig roasting. Phad, recognizing his now spitted nemesis, was pleased. There was *poi*, chicken *fa fa*, fresh coconut water, chocolate cake, croissants, and baked and steamed fish, including tuna and *mahi mahi*. Lorretta and Henri had prepared several special rice and potato dishes and several platters of *boeuf bourguignon*. I hadn't had that since I cooked it along with Julia Child during a rerun of one of her old shows. Henri's version was decidedly more successful than mine. All around us, while we enjoyed large platters of delicious victuals, children danced, old women played cards, and teens flirted.

Though we were tired and sated, Anna Marie, who had stayed quite near us throughout the feast, said it was time to cleanse us and give thanks for our successful journey. Emere, Gertrude, Anui, Lygia and I followed her to her house. There she required that we strip away all of our tattered and sweat-stiffened clothing. She bathed us with lime leaves and water while we stood on the beach in front of her place. She threw slices of ripe mangoes on the water while thanking the stonefish for its help. Then she brought out fresh, beautiful pareos for each of us and put a wreath of lime leaves on our heads.

She had prepared a cool room, with a lovely clicking overhead fan, for us. It had five small beds each with bright sheets and coverlets. She bade us rest, and we slept for a solid twenty hours.

When we awoke, around eleven in the morning, Anna Marie served steaming cups of café au lait and croissants delivered early that morning by Henri and Loretta. We had one more thing to do. Anui had carefully carried the birds, still packed in their nests, to Anna Marie's. We told Anna Marie about them and let her have a peek. Because she had raised chickens in the past, she still had a couple of oversized hen houses and a large fenced area beside her yard. We all spent the afternoon repairing the fence, cleaning the hen houses, and making certain that there were plenty of grasses and other plants that would give the birds choices in habitat and nesting material. Then came the problem of food. We didn't know what an "extinct" bird would eat, but, after a few Google searches, we decided that any small vertebrate or crustacean would probably be okay. We gathered what we could and the birds ate gratefully.

Of course we had had to destroy all of their nesting materials and clean the birds and their eggs thoroughly. The birds squawked. We treated all of what had been associated with the birds and come with us from Mauntaerae like hazardous material and deposited all the waste in a blue metal drum that had previously been used for noni juice. We marked big nuclear symbols on the barrel and sent it via the next cargo ship to hit the quay, bird poop and all, to the *Commissariat à l'Énergie Atomique* in Paris. They would know what to do with it.

A rainstorm came in around four in the afternoon, just after we put the birds into their new home. The sun shone through the rain and there was a triple rainbow over the lagoon and a pod of dolphins was playing.

That evening, when we looked in on them, the female bird was busily assembling a little home around the male bird who sat placidly on the pair of eggs we had laid gently in a grassy chamber.

CHAPTER XXXXIV

Farewell to Moa Nui

*What a lovely, tanned, energetic rascal I saw
running on the beach today.
He was lithe and ran like a leopard. Curiously, he had not a hair
on his sweaty head.*
From the Personal Journal of Fiona Elizabeth Kelly

All was back to normal. Even the sign on a storefront in Besoin for The Psychic Barber had been taken down. Nobody was interested in psychic anything, at least for the time being. Aunties laughed about their tattoos, compared them with glee, and offered unused tampons to younger women via notes on the Snack Shack bulletin board. There were other things to gossip about, new love affairs to consider, and fishing to do. It was time for me to go home. I would miss Moa Nui and my pals, but I had made the rounds, said my goodbyes and was ready to start packing.

It was hot. I put on my bathing suit, took a quick dip, and then got to work. As I was wrangling my sixteen packing cubes into my rolling duffle, putting my lotions and shampoos into zip lock bags, and making certain I'd grabbed all my plug adapters from the wall sockets, the women from next door, the Americans, hollered at me. One with lots of curly hair came to the edge of the wall that separated our properties. She was smiling broadly. She had managed to get a pretty good tan since I'd been gone.

"We haven't seen much of you lately," she said. Well, no. And, truth is, they hadn't seen much of me at all. I wasn't there to frolic or socialize. I walked toward the wall—no need to seem aloof—but I remained noncommittal regarding my whereabouts. Clearly, they had missed out on what everyone else on the island knew about. I suppose not speaking the languages and staying pretty much inside their own compound, they wouldn't have had a clue. I smiled.

"We're having a few people over tomorrow and wondered if you'd care to join us. We're making a big lasagna and sauce and meatballs. It will be delicious!"

She did cast a curious eye over my arms and legs. She was, however, polite enough not to ask. For although I was well rested by now, my body was covered with scratches, and I had swellings as big as ping pong balls all over my arms and legs from insect bites. My bathing suit hid nothing.

At first I thought to decline. Then I thought again. Why not? They seemed a funny lot, and, in any case, since I was leaving in two days I wouldn't be obliged to return the invitation or feel a need to develop a real relationship with the household. Still, I wouldn't spend the last afternoon on Moa Nui without my own friends.

"I'd love to come," I said, "but I'm afraid it is my last full day here and I'd want to spend it with my local friends."

There was a pause and then, "Oh, no problem. How many?"

"Oh four, maybe five," I said. Emere, Lygia, Anui, Gertrude, and maybe Anna Marie. I ticked them off in my mind, wondering if they'd be at all interested in lasagna.

There was another pause. "That's fine. We'll make a bit more than we had planned. Around 1 o'clock?"

"I'll bring chicken *fa fa*," I added. She looked puzzled. "Don't worry, you'll love it."

We hid the damage the best we could, but we were still noticeably scruffy. Lygia had horrible sunburn, being of Celtic stock. I had sunburn but had managed a daily slather of SPF 40, and most of my part of the adventure had been under the tree canopy. Lygia, meanwhile, had been running about on the beach with practically no clothes on. She had burns in places I didn't know one could burn. Nobody else had that problem, of course, though Anui and Gertrude and Emere were about three shades darker than we when set out.

Still, everyone agreed that meatballs, at least, would be great. And why not socialize with these Americans? We agreed not to mention anything of our trip. These women didn't know the local gossip, and it would be of no benefit to them to hear now what had been going on. They wouldn't have known about the walking washing machines or the tattoos or the group menstruations, and they may not even have noticed the big to do at the quay. We would keep it that way.

Emere left her musket home along with her bush hat. She brushed and twisted her lovely hair and put it back into its long braid. Lygia washed and fluffed her shortish, light hair and put on a new tank top she had purchased at the market. Even the extra-large didn't quite contain her ample bosoms. With a frangipani in her hair and a touch of lipstick from Emere's stash, she was presentable. Anui put on a clean shirt and pair of pressed shorts. He brought his wife, Marie, too. They didn't want to be apart again for a long time.

Gertrude had undergone yet another renovation in the couple of days since moving in with Emere. She had washed and cut her hair, scrubbed her body, and generally clipped and pruned herself. She wore one of Emere's lipsticks, "Menacing Magenta" I think she called it. She was actually a very attractive fifty-something, though still damned intimidating. It was something about those eyes, and the tattoos suggested her wild side. She was excited to meet a bunch of Americans. She had many questions to ask. I didn't understand why at the time.

I bought a new pair of earrings in the market and put a silk flower in my red hair. Aside from the ping-pong ball bites, I looked pretty darn good. Anui and wife, Emere, Lygia, and Gertrude came to my house first. Marie brought beautiful flowers wreaths for each of us to wear on our heads. Anna Marie arrived last. She brought some shell necklaces as gifts for the Americans. We giggled and fussed with each other and then crossed over to the other compound via the beach. We knew we all looked absolutely stunning. Emere grabbed the chicken *fa fa* as we headed for the other compound. We arrived just at one.

I led the pack up to the waiting group. They were tanned and seemed excited to see us. They each wore a colorful pareo and lots of black pearl jewelry. They'd been shopping. The smells coming from the kitchen were exquisite. There, behind the counter, was a slim bald fellow I'd seen running that morning. He was cooking the dinner. He wore a broad, welcoming grin.

"Hello," I said to everyone. "Thanks for invite." Emere held the chicken dish out and one of the women placed it on a set and waiting table.

"Yourroona," the curly headed one said.

The runner made a quick, surreptitious gesture from behind the counter. He wanted me to come closer.

"You don't recognize me?" he said.

I looked closely into his slim cheeked, chiseled face. He had big, friendly eyes, a Romanesque nose, and prominent jawbones.

He put a dishtowel over his pate. Everyone else was busy chatting in the other room. No one paid us any attention.

"Picture me with hair and a moustache," he said.

It didn't take long to see the fellow I used to know when I made the towel stand in for hair.

"Oh. I get it. What the hell are you doing here?" I whispered.

We had worked together on a case in Bulgaria many years ago. He'd shaved his head and face and lost about thirty pounds. What was his name? Mort? Stuart? Something like that.

He reached into the little pocket of his silk running shorts. He pulled out a flash drive.

"I was sent to find you," he said. "Long story."

"You must be joking," I said.

"Nope. You're needed. Go home, get some rest, read this, then get on a plane."

He went back to stirring a sauce and I dipped a spoon into the thick, rich gravy, drew it out, and licked it. All very innocent.

"How about a martini," the curly head offered from across the room. She was, clearly, the hostess.

I left the kitchen. Mort or whatever his name is got out some ice. We shuffled around speaking our names to one another. Everyone kissed everyone else on both cheeks, and said in unison, "We'd love one. Maruuru roa." Then we all broke out in truly joyful laughter.

We were really home.

Epilogue

It was hard to leave. The gang came to the airport with me the next day, and so did the Americans. They weighted me down with shell necklaces and kissed my cheeks until they tingled. I must admit, I wept a bit. We all vowed to see each other again.

I stayed in touch with everybody, and what I didn't hear directly, I heard via email and Facebook grapevines.

Lygia went home to Fogo Island shortly after I flew out. Her goats and bees were delighted to see her, as were the old aunts and uncles who still maintained their homes in the antiquated, quaint fishing villages. But things were changing quickly. A well to do former Fogo Islander had moved back with extravagant plans for developing the place. The blueprints had been approved for a three hundred-room hotel that would be build on one of the best beaches. There was already a restaurant that served portions of plated food for which no Islander would dream of spending ten dollars, much less thirty. The island had been named a top destination for the year by the New York Times thanks to some glad-handing on the part of developers and friends of friends. Very oddly shaped "studios" were being constructed here and there and advertised as spots for "artist residencies," destroying the local scenery, Lygia thought. It was true, she had to admit to herself, that many had left during the Smallwood era and that the island needed a boost to keep it from becoming uninhabited all together.

Nevertheless, none of these plans for Fogo sat well with Lygia. She brought her goats and bees to a sister's farm in New Brunswick, packed a few clothes and her cello, and bought a one-way ticket back to Moa Nui. Another island, another life. She had a little money left over from the sale of her house and property and invested it in a coffee house cum wine bar. She engaged Gertrude as chanteuse and barista and together they decorated the place with colorful fish lures, oyster shells, and flowing pareos. In fact, one of the specialties of the house was edible fish lures, made of spun sugar and decorated to resemble octopus skirts. They were a big hit with tourists, who often bought a dozen or so to take back home. Their menu featured croissants and baguettes made by Henri and Loretta.

Lygia and Gertrude played and sang nightly in long, colorful, matching gowns. Sometimes, Lygia played original concertos. Gertrude told and retold the story of our journey with the chants she had composed en route. She embellished liberally, and rewrote the worst of the lot composed en route. Editing came hard for her. She liked the immediacy of her first drafts. Tourists loved her, no matter how awkward her verse, and the story of our adventures became famous throughout the region because of Gertrude. Gertrude occasionally accompanied her chants with an eight string Tahitian ukulele.

The pair made absolutely no profit from their endeavors, but covered expenses and lived frugally in an old bungalow surrounded by a lovely garden of Tahitian ginger, papaya, and coconut palms. They relied on their very sensible government sponsored health care. It provided all the assistance they would ever need as they grew older.

Lygia followed the news of Fogo's development but had no inclination to leave Moa Nui. Gertrude never had the urge to go back to the mountains, but she finally told Lygia, who told me (with Gertrude's permission), that Henrietta Poussiere had been her mother. Henrietta had left the Island in the late 1940s—that much we knew—but what we never knew for certain was that indeed Henrietta had a local lover, gave birth to a beautiful daughter (long-boned from the beginning, like herself), and had kept all this secret fearing the reprobation of her professional colleagues. The daughter was around two years old when she left. So Gertrude really was a little over 60 years old.

It was true that Gertrude's father had died and, with her mother absent, she had been left in the care of traditionally minded and trained elders, both of whom were Henrietta's informants. Of course, as some us guessed, most of what Henrietta had been told and written about was untrue. People made up elaborate stories to please her and to help her with her career goals.

The local women had particular fun spinning tales about their monthly periods. They had, for generations, used their periods to get out of a week a month of work. They used these times to play games, tell stories, eat food someone else had cooked, and keep their husbands at bay by pretending to be "impure." The stories they told Henrietta suggested the need for isolation, elaborate costuming, and cross-dressing during full moons. They told her that they were required to walk backwards up *femme robuste* as part of their coming of age ceremony. These stories they staged (with much glee) often enough that Henrietta, starry-eyed and imagining the reception her monograph would receive, did not question a word.

All the locals also knew about her ridiculous Global Ignorance method and conspired together to scream complete and elaborate lies at her. They genuinely liked her, but they didn't tell her anything that would allow an invasion of their privacy or publication of what they considered either personal or sacred. They all believed that this career Henrietta had chosen was rude beyond belief. Gertrude, as she grew up, was told about the staged ceremonies and about the fun the women had making up "traditional" costumes. She was always eager to meet Americans, because she longed to know more about what her mother might have been like. Gertrude had no idea I would know of Henrietta. We exchanged some crazy letters and emails about all this.

Between other jobs, I did a search of Poussiere's archived research materials and found a wonderful collection of stories she'd collected in New Mexico. Gertrude flew to Olympia and together we edited and published a beautiful volume of this work and called it *The Romance of the Village of Solución: Tales Collected by Henrietta Poussiere*

Anui was extraordinarily happy with his wife Marie and their two children. They decided that it was appropriate for them to renew their marriage vows and make a public declaration of their love. They asked Anna Marie, who had a certificate of ministry from the Universal Life Church and could officiate at weddings, to prepare a solemn but understated ceremony. Most of the islanders witnessed.

The couple lived on a motu off the far side of the island and grew watermelon for market. Anui fished in the lagoon and his wife made dresses and packaged chicken *fa fa* and poi for sale on Sunday mornings in town. They had a small pickup truck that they left on the island side. Each Sunday early they piled their canoe full with the ripe melons, handmade clothing, coolers full of food, and the children, and paddled to shore. They transferred everything to the pickup and drove to town. They always stopped for a coffee at Lygia and Gertrude's place before going home. Marie, Lygia, and Gertrude became great friends. Marie took up button accordion so that she could play with the other women on occasion.

Emere sometimes joined the group for coffee. Her life didn't change much, but she did decide, after our big adventure, to write a book about her grandmother. She sent me a note when she discovered that the kakae we had found was not the omen bird she had remembered being told about. Apparently, our bird was always considered a sign of good luck. She admitted that she had often experienced vasovagal syncope and that, in the excitement of the climb and seeing the bird long thought extinct, she had had one of the fainting spells associated with the condition. It had not been a spell or a charm or anything particularly mysterious that had happened to her. Nevertheless, she said, she was glad of Aban's assistance. It was comforting to have the attention.

We heard infrequently from Aban, who sent a message general delivery to Moa Nui about a month after our return. Anui picked it up and sent telephone numbers and addresses of all of us to him. He called Emere once to see how she was and said he was moving to Kelantan, Malaysia, where he still had some family. There was some seasonal construction work to be had there. He used Emere's post office box number to send messages to all of us, so we received occasional cards with pictures of beaches and turtles and exotic drinks, but he didn't write much.

About a year out, he sent a photograph of himself. He was dressed in beautiful blue garments, including a baju melayu shot through with gold threads. He had a kain sarong looped round his waist. On his head was a beautifully embroidered songkok. Next to him was a solemn looking young woman who was queenly in her baju kurung and filigreed golden crown. Aban looked serious, too. They were sitting on a kind of throne, as required during the bersanding ceremony. They were "royalty," if only for a day. On the back, he wrote that he was married now and that this was a formal wedding picture. He said he was very happy. We all hoped to hear more soon. When we did, he had taken a job in Malaysia working for the United Nations. He had a grand house in Kuala Lumpur and a Mercedes sedan.

Phad settled back to life with Henri and Loretta, though he made his rounds. He loved lazing about listening to Lygia and Gertrude sing through the night and accepting offerings of day old croissants. Gertrude always had a bag of kibble from which to treat him and they kept a large bowl of water next to the ice cream cooler.

The *Gallirallus pacificus* thrived under special, watchful care. It became a symbol of regeneration and possibility for everyone on Moa Nui. It is featured on the Moa Nui five franc postal stamp

And me? When I got home, I fed my cat. Lucretia had missed me, but not that much. She really had grown to prefer the house sitter in my absence. I got a nuzzle and a piercing scream (something I really didn't need to remind me of my recent traumas), and then she settled back on her couch rug and went to sleep. I unpacked my bags and made a list of things I would need to replace before I set out for my next job, already pending. Insect repellent, socks, Band-Aids. Really, a whole new first aid kit seemed in order. My toothbrush was pretty grungy. I had used all of my little travel shampoos, conditioners, and toothpastes. My iPod needed new ear buds. I'd managed to rip the cord in two. I had a few holes in my favorite tank top. My boots were a mess from all the washing and rewashing. I had a hard time even getting them back through customs check. The clerk wanted to know if I'd recently been around livestock. Well, technically, no. It seemed I could spring for a new pair of Keene walking shoes and hope that I wouldn't need to scale any mountains in the near future. I'd look for a good sale. My supply of cleansing tissues was still pretty good. I'd held on to my water bottle in spite of it all.

With all that preparatory "housecleaning" completed and my bags and suitcase brushed and packed away, I carefully unwrapped the one souvenir I brought home from Moa Nui. I placed it gently on the large mantle over the fire place between family pictures and my copy of *The Red Book: Liber Novus by* Carl Gustav Jung. The little memento reminds me every day of what we accomplished. It is a walnut-sized, lustrous, snake head cowrie shell that I picked up on the beach just before I boarded my plane.

Acknowledgments

I have, in some instances, borrowed or adapted certain motifs and themes from pan-Pacific histories, legends, and events. My thanks to the storytellers who have recounted versions of these wonderful tales.

I owe a thanks to Karen Aqua and *Ground Zero/Sacred Ground*, the animated film she made as commentary on the Mogollon cultures of the American Southwest and the first atomic explosion at the Trinity Site in New Mexico. I grew up in the nuclear age and have been touched repeatedly by the devastation it has wreaked on people, both as weapon and source of energy. My most direct brush with the power of atomic energy was in July of 1962. I witnessed the explosion of a 1.44 megaton nuclear bomb called Starfish Prime. I was in Hawaii, where lights and televisions failed and power lines fused, according to one report. Satellites were disabled by radiation. This was a high altitude test conducted by the Defense Atomic Support Agency and the Atomic Energy Commission. A Thor rocket launched the bomb and the explosion took place 250 miles above Johnston Island in the Pacific. The "official" description of the phenomena visible in the sky up to 1400 miles away matches closely what I saw:

> "…a brilliant white flash burned through the clouds rapidly changing to an expanding green ball of irradiance extending into the clear sky above the overcast. From its surface extruded great white fingers, resembling cirro-stratus clouds, which rose to 40 degrees above the horizon in sweeping arcs turning downward toward the poles and disappearing in seconds to be replaced by spectacular concentric cirrus like rings moving out from the blast at tremendous initial velocity… As the greenish light turned to purple and began to fade at the point of burst, a bright red glow began to develop on the horizon at a direction 50 degrees north of east and simultaneously 50 degrees south of east expanding inward and upward until the whole eastern sky was a dull burning red semicircle 100 degrees north to south and halfway to the zenith obliterating some of the lesser

stars. This condition, interspersed with tremendous white rainbows, persisted no less than seven minutes. [1]

That experience, when I was nineteen years old and headed for the Sarawak, a Crown Colony on the Island of Borneo, heralded, for me, a new awareness of the horrors of war and the dangerous follies of men and governments. As a child, who had been drilled in elementary school to hide under a flimsy wooden desk should the Russians come, it gave me no joy to watch this "light show" that seemed to thrill so many that long ago summer in the Pacific.

Thanks to the Warumpi Band from the Northern Territory, Australia for the original of the song, *My Island Home.*

Thanks to Carl Chew and his work. His images inspired the idea of the Moa Nui stamp featuring the rehabilitated kalae bird.

Thanks for "Kilter Line Prophecy and Liberation Astrology" goes, in part, to Rob Brezsny. I first used the term "Freewill Astrology" for Anna Marie's practice. I thought it was my creation. Then I realized it is the title of a horoscope column in *The Weekly Volcano,* an alternative newspaper for Olympia and Tacoma, Washington. Brezsny has a copyrighted web page called *Rob Brezsny's Freewill Astrology.* Thus, I changed the name of Anna Marie's business.

Thanks to Joseph Campbell, whose work I studied many years ago, for teaching me that we can all have journeys and that we can all return with something that nourishes our world. He also taught me that even real heroes can have a thousand faces.

Thanks to H.P. Lovecraft and his mythos and fertile imagination for an understanding of what is really horrible and how to put it into words.

Thanks to Edgar Allen Poe for takili-li and the great story, *Narrative of A. Gordon Pym.*

---

[1] "A quick look at the technical results of Starfish Prime compiled and approved by Francis Naxin, staff, Los Alamos Scientific Laboratory. August, 1962.

Thanks to Chief Dan George for his life and work and the inspiration he provided to Gertrude.

Thanks to J. S.C Bach, of course.

Thanks to Jane Siberry for her musical inspirations, especially the song *One More Colour*. Some of her lyrics ought to be used in every writers' workshop. They show us how to get out of our "boxes," both as authors and people.

I often write to music to invoke a rhythm or a mood for my work. I listened to Siberry's albums while writing this book. She helped me to remember to think about point of view and vision. I listened to AC/DC. I listened to operas. Whatever seemed right for the day.

Thanks to George Peter Murdock, the anthropologist, whose real work is alluded to in the text.

Thanks to H.G. Wells and *The Time Machine* and *The Island of Dr. Moreau*. Wells is a longtime favorite and wonderful writer who created peculiar, troubling worlds and in so doing raised compelling questions we've not yet answered.

Thanks to Dame Kiri Te Kanawa and Mussorgsky, both of whom are mentioned in the text.

The drawing of the Gallirallus pacificus that appears in the Moa Nui stamp on this book's cover was created by Johann Reinhold Forster and copied by his son, Georg. The extinct bird was spotted and described by Forster during James Cook's second voyage to the Pacific. It is dated 1773.

My apologies to anyone else whose work I've alluded and whom I've forgotten to thank.

And many thanks, finally, to the dear friends whose love and charm has entered into this work and inspired my life in so many ways. You are always there for me. I appreciate it more than words can tell.

Nuclear Testing in the South Pacific

I read recently that perhaps as many as one thousand people from the Marshall Islands have moved to Spokane Washington. Why? Some of these moves are in consequence of the rising ocean level due to climate change. But there is more. From 1946 to 1958, the United States carried out sixty-seven "atmospheric" nuclear tests in the Marshall Islands. The well publicized fifteen megaton "Castle Bravo" was detonated on March 1, 1954, at Bikini atoll. Bernice Ralpho, now of Spokane, says poor health is common in the Marshall Islands. There are high rates of cancer and birth defects, she told a reporter in 2011. Plants and livestock just "aren't right." In 1956, the Atomic Energy Commission dubbed the Marshall Islands the, "most contaminated place in the world."

The fictional Moa Nui suffers potential environmental degradation from very real and known sources. The French from 1966-1996 in French Polynesia carried out a series of both atmospheric and underground nuclear tests. More than 170 tests were conducted. The damage to one atoll is well documented. The potential risk of more testing in the region to human and animal life is astronomical.

Disclaimer

This book is a work of fiction. Any resemblance to real people or real islands is unintentional. Characters, incidents, events, places, and such are drawn from the author's overactive imagination. Of course this imagination is informed by her own life, experiences, places she has been, and the many people she has known. However, there is no intention here to portray actual people, actual places, or actual events. No one other than the author is responsible for the content.